ROGER WILLIAMS

Mark Ammerman

Illustrated by
Kit Wray and Mark Ammerman

BARBOUR
PUBLISHING, INC.
Uhrichsville, Ohio

A godly heritage is a precious possession and a treasure worth digging for. This small book, a nugget from the motherlode, is affectionatley dedicated to Tony, Leslie, Conor, Jandy, Ryan, Kevin, Bethany, and Jonathan: the great, great, great, great, great, great, great, grandchildren of a truly great man.

© MCMXCV by Barbour Publishing, Inc.

ISBN 1-55748-761-8

Published by Barbour Publishing, Inc.
P.O. Box 719
Uhrichsville, Ohio 44683
http://www.barbourbooks.com

Member of the
Evangelical Christian
Publishers Association

Printed in the United States of America.

INTRODUCTION

Imagine a world without TV, McDonald's, packaged snacks, cars, bicycles, roller blades, microwaves, electric lights, hot showers, aspirin, deodorant, sneakers, T-shirts, contact lenses, computers, telephones, machine guns, or nuclear missles.

Imagine a nation where only one kind of church is legal, and where it is dangerous to say that you believe in something different. Where the law says you must go to church each Sunday, and where the king or queen or bishop tells everyone how to live. Where people can be thrown in prison for the wrong reasons without any trial. Where the government takes your money whenever it wants to. Where school lasts from sunup to suppertime, if you get to go at all. Where books are only allowed if the king's book-checker says so.

This is the world of Roger Williams as a boy. This is England in the beginning of the 17th century.

But people then were not much different than they are today. They worked and played and laughed and prayed, just like we do. They went to see Shakespeare's plays in theaters. They enjoyed live musical concerts, or they made music themselves and sang together to pass the time. They told stories.

They watched puppet shows and parades and went to fairs. They played cards, ran in races, and had other competitions. They went out to eat and drink at inns and brew-houses or at the homes of friends. Sometimes everyone was invited to a feast at the house of some rich man. They made their own fresh bread or bought it from others who made it. They made pies and cakes and candies. They drank tea and milk and beer. When they traveled long distances, they walked or rode horses or donkeys. Sometimes they rode on wagons or carriages pulled by animals, or in ships and boats. They built buildings as tall as they could, and bridges as long as they could. They used wood and stone and brick and metal and glass. They built stoves and ovens or cooked over fires, and they used salt and ice to preserve foods. They had doctors and dentists. They made many kinds of clothes by hand and enjoyed various fashions. They sent letters by messengers or by friends who were traveling. Soldiers were sometimes policemen and sometimes armies. They used muskets, swords, pikes, bows and arrows, and cannons. They marched or rode on horses.

Even with only one legal church in England, some people still had the courage to worship God differently. Some people still preached about Jesus even when the Church told them not to. Many people knew the Bible and loved the Lord. Many people began to believe that God would help them to rule their own country without a king. Many people tried to start good laws that gave others rights that could be protected. Some people went to school and then to college. They studied math and the Bible and different languages. There were books and pamphlets for those who could read. The King James Bible was first published during this time, and many good Christian books were available.

The capitol of England was London. Roger Williams was born there. It was a very big, very crowded, very busy city, full of buildings and people and animals. Even London Bridge had houses and stores built upon it. The King lived in London, too, and all the offices of his government were there.

In the countryside, the farms of the poor, the estates of the rich, and the little towns of the villagers were very busy too.

Now, imagine a world where there are tall trees and clear rivers that go on and on for endless miles. Under those trees are wild animals of all kinds, and people who live in tents and houses made of poles and bark and animal hides. They have no clothes except small coverings of animal skins, and all they have for cooking and hunting is made of wood, stone, bone, or shells from the rivers and sea. They plant corn and a few other vegetables. They hunt and fish and go to war. They cook over open fires. Their homes are heated the same way, and there is a hole in the roof to let out the smoke. They drink water. They sometimes kill and eat each other. They fight with knives and spears and clubs and bows and arrows. They believe in many different false gods and spirits, and live in fear of them all. They don't know who Jesus is, and Satan has them bound in darkness. When they are sick, their doctors make medicines from things that grow; and the doctors try to convince the spirits to take the sickness away. They have "sachems" (kings) who rule over them, and they have laws and customs that they pass down from generation to generation. Boys and girls grow up to be just like their parents in everything. They have no schools and no books. But even though life is often cruel and hard, they have a natural love for their families and friends. They laugh and they play. They tell stories and sing songs. They have races and competitions.

These people are the Indians of the great northeastern forests of America. They have lived this way for a long time.

On the edge of these savage forests, along the shore of the Atlantic Ocean, stands a handful of small English villages surrounded by walls made of wood from the trees of the forest. Soldiers with muskets and cannons guard the walls. There are a few nice houses in each village, but most are not much better than the homes of the Indians. They are furnished with items brought from England. In every village there is a church or meeting house where the people gather to worship the Lord. The town is ruled by magistrates and a governor who are elected by the members of the church. Food is scarce, and the people have to hunt and farm and fish like the Indians. Often they trade their English tools and trinkets for food from the natives. Sometimes another ship comes from across the ocean bringing supplies and more people. Life is much harder than it was in England. There is much sickness and death. There is much sorrow and the longing for things that are old and familiar. But the people are quickly learning how to live in this New World. And above all, they are learning to truly trust God. So there is much joy as well—deep joy amidst the pain and hardship of life in the wilderness. Sometimes they are able to share the Gospel of Jesus Christ with their Indian neighbors. Some of the Indians have begun to believe in the true God.

This is the world of Roger Williams when he was twenty-seven years old. This is America in 1630.

THE MORNING DAWNED AS MANY ANOTHER WINTER DAY.

1

A.D. 1611
One Winter Day

The morning dawned as many another winter day in the bustling London suburb of West Smithfield. Before the sun rose or the cocks crowed, hundreds of stoves in hundreds of cold, crowded wooden houses had been fired up against the damp March morning. Already at 5:00 a.m., the streets were filling up with the activity of a long, noisy day of business and play.

The year was 1611, and on Cow Lane—a narrow, winding street in the busy center of London's merchant district—an eight-year-old boy peered down from his third-story bedroom window at his waking neighborhood. His thick, dark hair was tousled and matted from a fitful night's sleep, but his thoughtful brown eyes were keenly awake as he surveyed the sights in the avenue below.

Down the crooked lane men and women faded in and out of the morning mist, as if in a dream. Some bore large woven baskets or burden-filled bags. Some carried satchels of papers or bundles of cloth. Some pushed wheelbarrows or rode carts pulled by donkeys. The muffled sounds of morning

9

greetings could be heard amidst the patter and clatter of foot and hoof and wheel on cobblestone. Shop doors opened and closed, as merchants began to haul out their wares for display.

Two stories directly below our young observer, James Williams—merchant taylor, buyer and seller of cloth—unlatched his own shop door and stepped out into the foggy Smithfield air. As he briskly started across the street, he suddenly stopped. Turning around, his gaze went upward toward the living quarters above his shop, and his eyes met those of his eight year old son.

"Good morning, Roger!" shouted Mr. Williams.

The boy pushed open his window a crack. "Good morning, Father."

"Roger, rouse your brothers if they aren't already up! Get dressed and have your breakfasts. We've work to do this day."

Then James Williams turned again and continued across the street and through the door of St. George's Inn. There, as was his habit each morning, he would hear any news of the night past and talk of the day ahead.

But there was something very out-of-habit about this morning. There were many unfamiliar faces in the inn. There were

"GOOD MORNING, ROGER!"

many strangers in the street. More women and children than usual. More donkeys and horses. More talk.

The scene from Roger's window was beginning to resemble the jumbled mass of party-goers who flocked to Smithfield once a year for St. Bartholomew's Fair. But this crowd was not a festive one. There was something in the faces of the people—something in the way they moved and spoke with each other—that evidenced troubled opinions and worrisome fears. Roger could see anger. Sorrow. Confusion.

"Today is the burning," said Roger aloud, as he turned toward his brothers, both already putting on their clothing.

"Today is the burning," echoed six-year-old Robert absently, as he tied his shoes.

"Yes, but that's not 'til noon," replied Sydrach, Roger's elder by three years. "We've plenty to do helping mother and father 'til then."

But it turned out that there was very little to do that morning, for folks were more intent on talk than work. And the more the streets filled, the more the people talked.

James Williams's shop was packed that morning with a small, sober group of men, all of whom Roger knew as friends of his father. All were merchant taylors like his father, and

"TODAY IS THE BURNING."

members of London's Merchant Taylors' Company. But they weren't discussing business. Roger and Sydrach sat on boxes in the back of the shop and listened.

"Legate is a heretic—the worst of his kind. It makes no difference that he's a fellow merchant taylor. He *deserves* to burn for his poisonous teachings!" declared a Mr. Fuller with a violent shake of his long grey hair and his thick, drooping mustache.

"He's a heretic, yes," agreed a Mr. Finch, whose clear blue eyes peered round about at his colleagues in the room. "And to preach that Christ is not God and not to be prayed to is poison indeed!"

Many heads nodded in sad agreement.

"But," continued Mr. Finch, "to turn a man into a torch for his opinions is just too..."

"Opinions, indeed!" interrupted Fuller with a sudden wave of his arm. "There is God's truth and there is the devil's falsehood! There is true doctrine, and there is heresy! The Church of England declares the doctrines of God, and we are to hold them to our hearts or perish in our sins!"

"I go along with the bit about God and the devil, but some of us fellows holds a different opinion in some matters than

"OPINIONS, INDEED!"

the Church of England, Mr. Fuller," said a Mr. Smythe quietly.

"Some of you Puritan fellows put too much on a man's *right* to 'hold an opinion'!" shouted Fuller.

"Opinions aside for a bit. Let's talk about the *man*," said Finch. "Two years ago when my shop burned, Legate sold me a quarter of his wares at no profit to himself. And all to help me back on my feet."

"And when my little Sally died," added a Mr. Johnson, sorrowfully and thoughtfully, "Bartholomew Legate was the first to come and pray with me. Though who he was prayin' to I guess I don't now know."

"And he was always first to speak well for the Merchant Taylors' Company, wasn't he?" furthered Smythe. "When Parliament forced us to help pay for colonization in Virginia, Legate sweetened it for us by getting them to promise one hundred acres of Virginia land to every contributor who had a trade."

"So, for which of these fine acts of citizenship and friendship does he stand condemned today!?" challenged Roger's father.

"For none of these, Father!" spoke a young voice from behind the band of businessmen. It was Sydrach.

"LET'S TALK ABOUT THE MAN."

"For none of these, but for heresy, Father," said Sydrach with conviction and yet with fear. "Mother says heresy is a sickness that spreads. And like a fire in a stable, it must be quickly quenched. Mr. Legate won't quiet, and he won't quit, so his candle must be put out."

"Sydrach!" exploded his father. "For all our talk of free opinions, I will have yours—and your mother's—in private from now on!"

The men laughed, but the boy shrank at his father's words. As he turned his head to the floor, his eyes became defiant.

James Williams continued to rail at his oldest son. "This candle you would rashly put out has burned warmly and kindly at our own table for years, Sydrach! He has been a welcomed guest in this home since before your birth! He prayed over you in your own cradle, long before he took it upon himself to dethrone Christ! Above all, though I hate his heresy for the heresy it is, he has been a *friend!*

"A friend," he quietly repeated, more to himself than to Sydrach. "A true friend."

And here Mr. Williams turned suddenly away from Sydrach, walked quickly from the circle of men, sat down upon a heap of cloth, covered his face with his hands, and

"HIS CANDLE MUST BE PUT OUT."

began to weep.

Roger had so seldom seen his father cry that he instantly ran to him and threw his arms around him. Sydrach stood up and, without looking at the men, left the room.

As the hour of the burning approached, all Smithfield (and a good deal of the rest of London) moved as one body through the parish of St. Sepulchre's toward the appointed place of execution.

James Williams and his family (his wife Alice, their oldest child Catherine, and their three sons) pressed forward in the crowd as far as they could safely go together. James, instructing the family to stick together where they were, pushed onward to where he caught sight of his friend, Bartholomew Legate. The condemned man was tied to a stake and surrounded by brush and wood.

"My God, Legate!" cried James above the deafening mob. "Call on the Savior even now! He hears! He truly hears!"

But Legate's own ears, cut off in partial punishment for his heresy, could not hear his colleague's admonition. As James stared upon the scene in disbelief and horror, Roger slipped silently beside him. He had followed his father through

"MY GOD, LEGATE! CALL ON THE SAVIOR EVEN NOW!"

the forest of arms and legs, and he reached now for his hand.

The moment had come, and the noise of the crowd quieted to the intermittent barking of dogs and the crying of babies. The charges of heresy were read, the sentence was pronounced, and the fire was lit. A mournful gasp escaped the crowd as though an eerie wind had suddenly filled the church courtyard, and the prayers of the burning man could be heard rising with the crackling flames. The heat of the fire and the brilliance of the noonday sun, with the growing roar of the deadly flames and the groaning crowd, made Roger dizzy. His father took him in his arms, and from this vantage point the young boy watched Bartholomew Legate die.

As the blackened form of the condemned man melted and collapsed within the center of the consuming pyre, Roger could bear it no more. "Mr. Legate! Mr. Legate! Mr. Legate!" he sobbed, as he buried his face in his father's cloak.

Mr. Legate had often carried Roger on his shoulders through these very streets. He had eaten and laughed and prayed at his father's table. He had sat Roger upon his lap and read to him from his father's Bible. In fact—and this was the memory that brought the bitterest tears—it was in those readings from the scriptures that Roger's young heart had

"MR. LEGATE! MR. LEGATE! MR. LEGATE!" ROGER SOBBED.

been turned toward Jesus, had opened wide, had believed. And yet this man no longer believed that Jesus was God, and so the fires of hell had broken loose from beneath the earth in Smithfield and consumed him. But no! These were not hell's flames. This fire was lit by man, and set to man, to kill a man. Did Jesus, who died for all, ever command such a thing? Roger was sure He had not.

As the crowd began to wander away into the streets and alleys of Smithfield, Roger and his father returned to their waiting family. Together they walked slowly and silently toward their home on Cow Lane.

Roger was the first to break the silence. "Father, should a good man be killed for having bad ideas?"

"Hush, Roger!" said his mother. "Mr. Legate denied the Lord's deity. He was fool enough to teach *others* his bad ideas. And now God is his judge."

"God will indeed be his judge, Alice, and I fear for the foolish man's soul. But *man* was his judge this day," countered James. "The Church was his judge. The King was his judge."

"Should not the King judge heretics, Father?" asked Sydrach, with a trace of a challenge in his voice.

THEY WALKED SLOWLY AND SILENTLY TOWARD THEIR HOME.

James ignored the challenge, but offered one of his own, "What if the *King* were a heretic, son? Who would judge *him*?"

"James!" fired Alice.

"Is the King a heretic, Father?" asked Roger.

"I did not say so. Only that he is not God," replied Mr. Williams.

At home, Roger pulled a book from his father's shelf and laid it open upon the kitchen table. It was Foxe's *Book of Martyrs*, a volume filled with stories and pictures of men and women who had been martyred for their faith in Christ. Judged and killed by kings and queens and bishops, most of them had been executed for simply believing something different than the kings and queens and bishops had told them to believe. Many of them had died right there in Smithfield, only a half-century before Roger was born.

He turned the familiar pages—pages known to all men, women, boys, and girls in England in those days—until he came to the story of a man named John Lambert. Lambert was burned at Smithfield in 1538, during the reign of Henry VIII. The picture on the page showed Lambert tied to the stake with the flames ascending. Lifting his burning hands, he was crying out, "None but Christ. None but Christ!"

IT WAS FOXE'S *BOOK OF MARTYRS.*

ROGER AND JON RAN TOWARD THE DOCKS.

"RIGHT HERE!"

Sepulchre's, says that we are wrong to cross the seas for gold or greed."

The boys sat down for a moment on the edge of the dock, legs dangling over the slow-moving waters of the dark Thames. Their minds wandered from the busy London riverside to a lonely land beyond the horizon, a land that was fast capturing the imagination of all England. A land that seemed to hold out promises and hopes that could only now be dreamed of.

"In my church at Austin Friars," said Jon, "everybody is talking of a bay above Virginia discovered by Holland."

"A new bay?" said Roger.

"Yes. It will be a Dutch colony, and not an English one. I don't know if I'd rather go to Virginia or to this New Holland," continued Jon.

"Since you are English *and* Dutch, I think you should visit *both*," said Roger. Then he jumped up and began to pace the dock, "Let's pretend that you are the Dutch Governor in that new bay, and I will be Captain Smith. Together, we'll go to visit King Powhatan, noble chief of the savage Indians. He'll capture us, but you will escape and go for help. Then

THEIR MINDS WANDERED TO A LAND BEYOND THE HORIZON.

Powhatan's daughter Pocahontas will rescue me from death, just as Captain Smith has written in his book about Virginia."

"If my sister were here, she could play Pocohantas," offered Jon.

Roger made a face and said, "Aw, she's always chasin' after me! Let's not mix our fun with *real* girls. And we can be our own Indians, too. C'mon, let's gather some gull feathers to make Indian hairbands."

The two boys scrambled down from the dock to the wet river's edge in search of props for their fantasy. Above them, in the street that ran beside the Thames, an older group of boys was parading homeward after a swim. When Roger and Jon emerged from the shadows beneath the pier, their hair was decked with feathers and their faces were smeared with "Indian paint" of Thames shore mud. They were waving make-believe Indian hatchets made of sticks and shouting made-up Indian war cries when they came face-to-face with the older boys.

"Ow? What 'ave we 'ere?" asked a self-appointed leader of the gang of swimmers. "Looks like some Virginia savages out for English blood!"

ROGER AND JON PRETENDED TO BE INDIANS.

The gang laughed, and so did Roger, but Jon shrank back a bit.

"We're on our way to Jamestown to re-capture Captain Smith," said Roger. "Do you want to play?"

The gang leader, a red-headed lad of about thirteen years, ignored Roger and stared at Jon. "Looks like *this* one is a *Dutch* savage and not a Virginian after all. 'Course there's not much difference, as we can all see, right mates?"

The older boys laughed again and pushed and ribbed each other. But Roger wasn't laughing now.

The red-head, looking straight at Jon, continued his verbal bullying. "So, little chief, just who does *yer* tribe worship, anyhow? The Lord a'mighty, or some 'foreign god'? D'you obey the Church of England, or d'you sacrifice to demons in yer stinkin' huts?"

The bully, though it sounded as though he were poking fun at Indian paganism, was actually ridiculing the religious traditions of the protestant Dutch community of Austin Friars (about which, since he had never been inside their church or their homes, he actually knew *nothing*). This group of Dutch and French families had fled to England to escape re-

"WE'RE ON OUR WAY TO JAMESTOWN."

ligious persecution and had obtained unique permission from the King of England to worship as they chose. But because their faith and life was different from their English neighbors, they were often made fun of, hooted, or abused in the streets.

Roger stepped closer to the gang of jeering boys. Though he was smaller than some of them by nearly a foot, he was not afraid of them. He knew most of them by name. They were his neighbors, and some were his friends.

"Jack Dickens," said Roger, to the chief bully, whom he knew to be a friend of Sydrach's and a member of his own church. "Why can't you let us alone? Reverend Edwards says the Austin Friars worship Jesus too. They just go about it a bit different, but that's no reason to be mean to them. Jon is a Christian, and he's my friend."

But Jack Dickens was in no mood to be moved by pious reasoning.

"Ow? And if 'e's your friend, then you must be just like 'im. You're both little savages, as yer faces plainly show! 'Ere! Back to the shadowy woods with ya!" said Dickens. He gave Roger a rough shove, and the nine-year-old tumbled

"ERE! BACK TO THE SHADOWY WOODS WITH YA!"

backwards over the cobblestones and fell at Jon's feet.

Jon was angry. He had been beaten before because of the faith of his family. He had run through alleys to escape many a larger bully or gang. He didn't run this time. As Roger got slowly up, rubbing a badly bruised elbow, Jon scooped up a round stone and flung it straight at Jack.

It hit him square in the head. His legs went out from under him and down he went, as though he were a wooden pin knocked over by a bowling ball. A harsh cry went up from the older boys, and several of them pounced on Jon.

"Stop it!" shouted Roger, as he tried in vain to pull the boys off his friend. "Peter! Henry! Call off your mates!" he yelled to the other boys who were still standing by. But they kept their distance from the pile of flailing arms and legs.

By the time a couple of sailors heard the ruckus and broke it up, little Jon had been badly bruised and bloodied. And Jack Dickens was still unconscious in the street. When he was finally roused, he couldn't remember who he was or how he came to have such a marvelous lump on his forehead. His friends had to walk him home. But his father soon reminded him of his fine heritage and his good name, and he was shortly

IT HIT HIM SQUARE IN THE HEAD.

well enough to carry on his mischief as before.

Roger had to convince one of the swimmers, Henry Adams, to help him carry Jon to the Vanderhook house.

As they headed toward the Dutch quarter of Smithfield, Roger gave vent to the fire of injustice that was burning in his bones.

"Why didn't you try to stop it, Henry?!" challenged Roger.

"Why didn't you just leave it alone when Dickens was only mouthin'?" argued Henry.

"Because Dickens was wrong! And so are you for bein' a coward about it. You know Jon is a Christian!" countered Roger.

"'Course I am," said Jon, weakly, in his own defense.

"We *all* are, Roger," said Henry. "So don't think s'much about it! Sydrach says you think too much and..."

"Sydrach doesn't think at all!" snorted Roger. "And if we're all Christians, then I guess we shouldn't be beatin' each other up, should we!"

When they arrived at the Vanderhook home, Mrs. V. was much upset to see Jon in such shape. But as she listened to their story, she took the time to look after Roger's arm as

"YOU KNOW JON IS A CHRISTIAN!"

well.

"God will bless you, Roger Williams, for your faithfulness to a friend," she said as she bandaged his elbow. "You have stuck closer than a brother to Jon today. I am proud of you, as your own mother and father should surely be. And thank you, too, Henry Adams, though you're old enough to have done a bit more than just bring home the wounded after the war!"

Henry Adams walked home that evening with his pride bruised and his conscience sorely challenged.

Roger Williams wandered back to Cow Lane with his heart aching, but his head held high.

"GOD WILL BLESS YOU, ROGER WILLIAMS."

"WHO IS THAT ATTENTIVE YOUNG MAN BACK THERE?"

3
A.D. 1617-1621
The Star Chamber

"Who is that attentive young man back there?" asked Sir Edward Coke quietly to his wife.

Lady Hatton leaned toward her husband in the pew and whispered, "Which young man, Edward?"

"To our right, two rows back. The one so wrapped up in the sermon and taking notes so nicely in shorthand," said Sir Edward.

Lady Hatton turned discreetly and let her eyes wander through the Sunday morning congregation at St. Sepulchre's Church. Then she looked for the lad in question, and promptly found him. Turning back, she faced the minister, but quietly answered Sir Edward. "That's young Roger, son of James Williams. Williams is a merchant taylor here in Smithfield. His wife is the former Alice Pemberton. Her brother, James Pemberton, was our Lord Mayor of London a few years back."

"Ah, yes. Thank you, dear," said Coke thoughtfully, as he turned his gaze toward the pulpit again. But his mind wandered from the message on God's kingdom to his own everpresent thoughts on the earthly kingdom and government of his native England.

Sir Edward Coke was Chief Justice of the King's Bench, the top judge in the land. At sixty-five years old, he was England's greatest and most famous legal expert. His clear eyes were used to noting details, and his keen mind was used to judging character. This Sabbath morning he was impressed with the apparent qualities of a young lad two pews back.

Roger was merely doing what was then required of all English schoolboys. Monday morning he would stand before the schoolmaster's desk to present a written outline on Sunday's sermon. He would be questioned about the biblical text that was preached, what it meant, and how it was to be applied to everyday life. Roger loved the scriptures, and he took a serious delight in this bit of homework. Having learned at an early age how to write in shorthand, he used it often when taking notes or jotting down his thoughts. He was very good at it.

After the service, while Roger was greeting some friends, Sir Edward approached James Williams.

"Master Williams," said Sir Edward, "Your son appears

SIR EDWARD COKE WAS CHEIF JUSTICE OF THE KING'S BENCH.

to be a pious young man with some talent in shorthand."

"Thank you, Sir Edward!" replied Roger's father, flattered by this unexpected appraisal of his boy. "His faith is a blessing to me and a reason for me to bless God. And his shorthand has served me well in my trade. It has served the Merchant Taylors' Company some as well."

"Perhaps it could serve the King and the country at large. I would like to employ the young man," said Coke. "I would like him to take case notes for me at court. In the Star Chamber."

"Employ him?" said a startled Mr. Williams.

"How old is he?" asked Sir Edward.

"He's fourteen," answered Roger's father.

"He'll do fine," was the reply.

Roger could barely take notes the first day, sitting in that large courtroom with the glittering stars painted upon its ceiling. In a long building behind Westminster Abbey in the heart of London, the Star Chamber sat at the edge of Roger's beloved Thames. Though he could walk home from there in half an hour, it seemed that he was a world away from his classroom in Smithfield. And indeed he was.

"EMPLOY HIM?"

ROGER WILLIAMS

This was not the working-class world of his merchant-dominated neighborhood; this was the world of politics and power. This was not the tap room of St. George's Inn where men's ideas and opinions flowed as freely as the beer; this was the judgment seat of a nation where the rights and consciences of men were too often strangled by the unchallenged power of the King's Court. This was not the docks in Smithfield where a lad could almost taste the freedoms that lay beyond the salty blue horizon; this was the room in which Bartholomew Legate had been sentenced to death for his religious beliefs.

Roger's awe of the lawyers dressed in scarlet faded as the days turned into months. But his respect grew for the great man who had hired him. And as the months turned into years, Sir Edward grew to love this gentle and intelligent young son of a merchant taylor. He loved him for his commitment to God's truths, his passion for justice, and his heart for mercy. He delighted in his insights on scripture, his thoughts on the court cases he was recording, and his opinions on the rights of the individual. Coke, himself, though a powerful and popular man of great service to the King, had already been imprisoned twice for speaking out in behalf of the rights of the

THIS WAS THE WORLD OF POLITICS AND POWER.

common man.

One night the old lawyer and his young disciple sat before a fire in Sir Edward's home. The judge's white beard seemed to glow in the firelight as he looked into Roger's bright face.

"What you say about freedom of religious conscience is quite true, Roger," said Sir Edward. "A man should be free before God to believe as his heart leads him. But if we all spoke our minds and demanded to live as we pleased, there would be chaos. God is not the author of chaos, but of order. He is not the author of license, but of law."

"But, Sir Edward, I am not saying we should live to please ourselves or to give in to the sin in our hearts. I am saying that we should be free under the law to worship God as we choose."

Roger rose from his chair and began to pace the room.

"Just last week," he continued, as the firelight threw his moving shadow upon the opposite wall, "the Chamber tortured, condemned, and threw an old man into prison for one heretical sentence that he wrote in a sermon that he never preached!"

"And if the court does not punish heresy, then how will the doctrines of the Lord remain pure?" challenged Sir

"WE SHOULD BE FREE. . .TO WORSHIP GOD AS WE CHOOSE."

Edward. "How can our nation remain free and be blessed by God if it allows His teachings to be twisted by every man's conscience?"

"Freedom does not come by the sword or the court," Roger replied. "Our Lord Jesus declared that only *he* can make a man free. So freedom comes by faith. And faith cannot be forced by either church or state, because true faith is a matter of the soul. It is between each man and God alone. So how can a nation be truly free or blessed by God if it does violence to the soul?"

"Would you have us put away our swords and be at the mercy of infidels, traitors, and rebels?" asked Sir Edward.

Roger shook his head emphatically. "No! The scriptures say the sword is rightly raised against those who lie or steal or harm their neighbor. But neither the sword nor the bonfire should ever be used to persecute a man for ideas. Even bad ideas!"

"Your words are always stimulating, Master Roger, but I must change the subject radically before we say goodnight. Please be seated, will you?"

Roger sat down.

Sir Edward looked into the flames for a moment and then

ROGER SHOOK HIS HEAD EMPHATICALLY. "NO!"

turned to Roger with a sincere and loving gaze. "Your faithful service to me these past four years, in the Star Chamber and in many an evening we've spent together, has been more than I can ever repay. You are like a son to me. And so I wish to do for you as I would for my own son. I want to send you on to preparatory school, that you might go on to Cambridge and to the ministry."

"I am honored, Sir Edward. Truly I am," said Roger. "But I have not served you for such privilege, and I am undeserving..."

"Nonsense, my boy! If anyone deserved the chance to serve God and the Church in this way, it is you."

"But father isn't well, Sir Edward, and I've been thinking he may need me by his side. And in his shop."

"I have spoken with your father, Roger. His heart for you is even as I have just proposed. And the Church of England, as much as our Puritan brethren may not agree with all her traditions, needs young men of faith and fire like you."

Sir Edward rose from his chair and placed his hand on Roger's shoulder. "Your schooling will start at Charterhouse within a month."

"YOUR SCHOOLING WILL START AT CHARTERHOUSE..."

JAMES WILLIAMS WAS DYING.

4

A.D. 1621
My Father, in Heaven

At his father's bedside, Roger prayed. James Williams was dying. He had been feverish for a week and barely able to eat for half that time. Breathing became increasingly difficult, as his weakened lungs strained painfully to pull air into his failing body. He could no longer sit up in bed. Today, he had hardly opened his eyes. And now the night was settling in.

"Father of mercies," Roger pleaded, "though Heaven is more to be desired than all lands and riches on earth, still I would have my father here with me longer. Oh, God of grace and life, what a sad world this is!"

Roger opened his father's Bible upon the bed, and turned the ragged pages until he came to the book of James. As his eyes passed slowly over the holy words, he stopped at a certain passage and read aloud,

" 'Be afflicted, and mourn and weep. Let your laughter be turned to mourning and your joy to heaviness.' "

His eyes swelled with hot tears, which he wiped upon the

bedsheets. Then he read on, " 'For what is your life? It is even a vapour, that appears for a little time and then vanisheth away.' "

Roger wept.

"Please, Roger, get some sleep," said a tender voice from the doorway. It was Catherine. She entered the room with a pan of water and began to gently wash her father's sweaty face with a cool, damp cloth.

"I can't leave him now, Catherine. I believe he may not see another morning. And then what shall we do? What is this life to be like without one who loved us so?"

Catherine ran her fingers through her brother's thick hair. "He loved us all, but he loved you most. It is your tenderness for Jesus that endeared you to him. Sydrach hates you for that, but perhaps the Lord will bring him to repentance."

Roger looked up into his sister's misty eyes. "Will Sydrach take good care of Mother and Robert while I am at school?" he asked.

"Oh, yes," answered Catherine. "He can handle the shop as well as Father. My husband Sam will also give a hand when needed. But I fear we'll lose some business. Sydrach is

"WILL SYDRACH TAKE GOOD CARE
OF MOTHER AND ROBERT?" ROGER ASKED.

too outspoken for the King. Father's Puritan friends may go elsewhere for their cloth. But we'll make out. Mother's relatives, the Pembertons, will help us if it comes to that."

"Sit with me," said Roger. "Pray with me for Father. For the family."

As the hours slowly moved toward a new dawn, Alice Williams quietly joined her two children in the watch. Elsewhere in the sad, silent house, Sydrach and Robert slept fitfully.

James Williams never awoke.

ALICE WILLIAMS JOINED IN THE WATCH.

"THE BIBLE *COMMANDS* US TO SEARCH THE SCRIPTURES!"

5
A.D. 1628
Laud, Have Mercy!

It was a late afternoon in May, and the students at Cambridge were on their daily "liberty" (a short period of free time before supper). In Roger's little room, three young men sat in heated conversation. A sharp-featured fellow named Jonas Lamb was loudly complaining about a recent hard turn of events.

"Seven years of our lives in preparation for the ministry! And now the high and mighty Charles the First declares by his 'Sovereign Power' that 'all further curious search into church doctrine be laid aside'! The Bible *commands* us to search the scriptures! And I'd like to *know* what a man's to preach if not *true doctrine*!" Lamb said bitterly.

"Seven years is an awfully long time to be climbing the Church stairs only to have the doors slammed in your face," said a stout, little man named Richard Goddard.

"The keys to those doors are in Bishop Laud's hands," said Roger. "He'll let us in *if* we promise to be obedient little

Anglicans."

"Laud is worse than King Charles!" snorted Goddard.

"And Charles is worse than King James was!" added Lamb.

"But it's Laud who is stirring the King up against the Puritans," continued Goddard. "If the Bishop weren't such a fanatic for the traditions of the Church of England, Puritan voices wouldn't be so severely silenced. All we want is to turn the Anglican Church more toward the Church of the Bible!"

"We don't need some fancy parish church to preach in," said Roger with a wave of his arm. "We can declare the Gospel in people's homes, in private meetings, in the streets if need be!"

The other men were silent for a moment. Then Goddard spoke again. "If we were to separate from the Church of England, then Laud would *really* be on our tails. How could we change things if we were religious outlaws? I think we must simply pray, and hope that God changes the King's heart."

Roger got up and began to pace the room. "*Martin Luther* was a 'religious outlaw'! Didn't God protect *him*? And didn't *he* change a few things?!" he argued. "None of us in this

"MARTIN LUTHER WAS A 'RELIGIOUS OUTLAW'!"

room would ever have heard the Gospel if he hadn't had the courage to stand up for the truth. If Laud wants someone to persecute, let's give him. . ."

There was a sharp knock at the door, and Roger opened it. It was the school's Master, Jerome Beale. Behind him in the hallway were two armed soldiers.

"Good afternoon, Mr. Williams," greeted Beale. He looked around the room at the others seated there. "Best be readying yourselves for the evening meal, men," he said.

"What's going on here?" asked Lamb, as he got up from his stool and stared out the door at the soldiers.

"Mr. Williams is to travel with these men to see Bishop Laud," replied Master Beale. "I am assured that he will be treated as a gentleman and will return to us shortly."

Roger and his friends could hardly believe their ears.

"Sit here, please, Master Williams," said William Laud, pointing to a large chair next to his own.

Roger sat down, and stared into the Bishop's dark green eyes.

"I went to Cambridge, too," said Laud. "An excellent school."

BEHIND MASTER BEALE WERE TWO ARMED SOLDIERS.

"Yes, sir, I am very grateful for my years within its walls," said Roger.

"As an alumnus, I have followed your academic progress," continued Laud, looking vacantly past Roger into the darkened corners of the spacious room. "Many of the students look up to you for your godly manner, and your ability to argue your. . .your convictions and opinions. Of course your sponsor, Sir Edward Coke, has set you an excellent example in these things."

Roger sat up in his chair, a proud gleam in his eyes. "A man of honor, wisdom, and piety; indeed a glorious light! Since my own father died, Sir Edward has often called me his son. Truly his instruction and encouragement have spurred me on in all that I do!"

"Of course, of course," said Laud, looking Roger in the face. "And Coke is a man who is not afraid to question tradition or authority when he sees a falsehood in it. Even if it means opposing the King."

"For this I love him most!" Roger replied.

"For opposing the King?" asked Laud.

"For opposing falsehood," said Roger.

"FOR THIS I LOVE HIM MOST!" ROGER REPLIED.

"But let's speak of Cambridge again," continued the Bishop. "Our college years seem to be a time when we're inclined to question the truths and traditions that we. . ."

"Bishop Laud," interrupted Roger. "I have spent most my life questioning traditions and searching for truth in the Scriptures. I believe it is the duty of every Christian to do so."

The Bishop stared at Roger grimly.

"May we get to the point for which you summoned me?" asked Roger.

"I will present the questions, Mr. Williams," said Laud.

Roger was silent.

"How do you spend your free time at the University, Mr. Williams?"

"Generally, in biblical studies and discussion," answered Roger.

"Have you ever been to a Separatist meeting?" queried Laud.

"Many times," said Roger. "Since I was a boy. Have you never been to one, sir?"

The Bishop ignored the question. "You've been taking your 'free-time biblical studies' in Smithfield, haven't you? At the

THE BISHOP STARED AT ROGER GRIMLY.

underground meetings of the Separatist Puritan leader Derek Baxter, haven't you? And you've even been *preaching* at some of those gatherings, haven't you?"

Roger said nothing.

"And you have spoken out against the King and his Church!" challenged Laud.

At this, Roger could not be silent. "The Church is *Christ's*, not the *King's*. Not the Bishops' nor the Elders'. Not yours nor mine," he replied.

Laud grew red in the face, and he blew air from his puffed cheeks. "You have denied the King's right to punish those who disagree with the Church of England!" challenged Laud.

"Weren't all Protestants, men just like you and me, judged 'heretics' when Bloody Mary was our Queen?" Roger argued. "When she burned those who disagreed with *her*, was it her 'Divine Right' to do so? Was it within her 'Sovereign Power'? Or did she do so out of her own human opinions and prejudices?"

Laud stood up. A big man even when seated, he seemed larger than himself when he was angry. He was getting very angry.

"THE CHURCH IS CHRIST'S!"

"*Mary* was the heretic, as you well know, Williams! She was a pawn of Satan and the Antichrist! But Charles is true King and true Christian! The Anglican Church is the true Church! And I am a true Bishop under God," Laud steamed.

"I am ordering you in the name of the King to cease your preaching against the crown! If you continue, you will stand at court on charges of treason!" continued the Bishop, standing over Roger and shaking a stiff finger in his face. "And as for your graduate ministerial studies at Cambridge, you might as well quit! Because you can forget about *ever* having a pulpit of your own!"

Now Roger was standing. The two men were face to face. Laud's fists were clenched. His body was tensed.

Roger opened his mouth to speak, but he stopped himself. Swallowing heavily and fighting back angry tears, he lowered his eyes to the floor. "Lord God, help me to hold my tongue!" he prayed within himself.

Laud slowly relaxed and then stepped back. For a long moment no one spoke. Then the Bishop quietly and coldly said, "You may go now."

"YOU MAY GO NOW," SAID THE BISHOP.

ROGER WILLIAMS

It was dark when Roger left the Bishop's house. As he started off on foot toward Cambridge, he became aware that he was being followed. Glancing back over his shoulder, he could see a man about his height, close behind but always in the shadows. Turning a corner near a noisy brew-house, Roger sank back into the cover of some dark bushes. Shortly, the man came around the corner, too. Stopping suddenly, he looked up and down the dimly lit street.

"Roger?" said the man, quietly at first, with his back to the bushes. Roger thought his voice was familiar, but. . .

"Roger Williams?" said the man again, more loudly this time, as he turned in yet another direction. And then, from the light that shone from the brew-house windows, Roger recognized his pursuer.

"Jon!" exclaimed Roger, stepping out from his hiding place.

"Whoah!" shouted Jon Vanderhook, stumbling backwards in surprise. "Roger! You *scared* me!" he said.

"As you scared *me,* you thief in the night! What are you doing coming after me like this?"

"We heard that Laud had sent for you, so I came to watch

ROGER SANK BACK INTO THE DARK BUSHES.

for you and to bring a message from your Separatist Puritan friends."

"Come! Walk with me, and tell me about it," said Roger. "I do hope it's good news after the trials of this evening! I've been accused of preaching against the King, Jon. And as long as Laud is Bishop, he will keep me from any pulpit within the Church of England."

Roger threw his eyes toward the starry heavens and shouted into the night sky, "*Let* the King be King, I say, and God bless him! But let the Church be the Church! There is room for only *One King* on the spiritual throne of thrones: *Jesus!*"

"Perhaps I do have good news for you," said Jon. "You may have your pulpit sooner than you think."

"Tell me, Jon!"

"Sir William Masham wants you for his chaplain."

"Chaplain of Otes Estate? 'Tis far better than a parish in London, Jon! And no Bishop can forbid it! Praise the Almighty, I'll take it!"

"PERHAPS I HAVE GOOD NEWS FOR YOU," SAID JON.

OTES MANOR IN ESSEX COUNTY

6
A.D. 1629-1630
Out of the Land

Otes Manor, in Essex County, was about ten miles outside London. Like many country estates of the time, it was a self-sufficient community. Within Masham's grounds, wheat was grown to provide bread for the household. Sheep were raised and flax was planted for the weaving, dying, cutting, and fashioning of clothing. Candles were crafted from peeled rushes dipped in tallow. There were barns and granaries, orchards and fields, animals and laborers. Within the Masham manor house, there was a wash-room, a folding chamber, a brew-house, a malt house, a dairy, a cheese loft, a buttery, a dry larder, and a pastry house. There were bedrooms, kitchens, baths, dining rooms, sitting rooms, a library, and a chapel.

A chaplain of such an estate, as Roger now was, was actually pastor of a private parish. His duty was to look after the souls of the entire household, from master and mistress to the servants who watered the sheep and fed the pigs.

Sir William Masham was a Puritan and a member of

Parliament. Jailed once for opposing a war tax decreed by the King, he was an outspoken voice for reform in both the Church and the government of England. His massive estate at Otes was a secret meeting place for many of the most powerful Puritans in Parliament.

But Parliament was a little *too* powerful for King Charles. It often disagreed with his decrees and too often passed laws in favor of the rights of the commoner. So in March of 1629, Charles put an end to Parliament. Roger was there with Masham in London when Parliament's old wooden doors were closed and locked by order of the King.

"What is happening to our nation?" said Sir William, as he and Roger rode home on horseback down the rutted highway toward Essex. "When a King takes the laws of the land into his own hands, who can be free from his long arm?"

"What is happening to the Church?" added Roger. "When a Bishop declares what prayers can be prayed and what prayers cannot, who can be free to worship God?"

"Roger, the Church is ever on your mind! But the Church itself is not free in England. She is under the thumb of non-Christian clergy and full of unrepentant sinners. I wonder

PARLIAMENT'S DOORS WERE CLOSED AND LOCKED
BY ORDER OF THE KING.

lately if she can ever be free," said Sir William.

Sir William suddenly spurred his horse on faster. "Follow me!" he called to Roger. Roger kicked his mare to catch up.

Sir William rode faster still, as the two men and their horses galloped neck and neck over the dusty road.

"It's a race we're in!" shouted Masham over the noise of the pounding hooves. "We must stay ahead of the King and his Bishop. We must preach the gospel while it is day, and ride long into the night if need be."

"But if we are always running, who will build or plant? There can be no fruits of righteousness if no one plants an orchard," replied Roger.

"'Tis truth you speak, Roger! Indeed, some must plant. But others must run!" shouted Sir William.

"And while we run from the King, where shall we run to?" asked Roger, ducking under a low-hanging branch as the horses thundered down the familiar lane.

"I did not say we should run *from* the King, only that we must stay *ahead* of him," yelled Sir William as the gates of Otes came into view. "But in so doing, perhaps we shall run to the sea. Perhaps we shall sail beyond the horizon. Perhaps

"IT'S A RACE WE'RE IN!" SHOUTED MASHAM.

we shall plant God's Vineyard and build Christ's Church in a land *beyond* the reach of England's corrupted Crown!"

" 'Your old men shall dream dreams,' " quoted Roger.

" 'Your young men shall see visions,' " returned Sir William. "You must *capture* this vision, young man!"

"You've been talking to Winthrop again, haven't you?" laughed Roger, reining his sweaty horse in front of the house.

The late July sun was still high over Sempringham Castle when the mud-encrusted figure of John Winthrop rode wearily up to its doors. The servant who let him in was surprised at his soiled appearance, and hurried to bring him water and a change of clothes. Winthrop gratefully washed his hands and face, but refused the clothes. He was anxious to begin the business for which he had ridden so far.

The servant led him down a long hall toward a massive pair of intricately carved doors.

Behind those doors sat a prestigious gathering of Puritan gentlemen: ministers and lords, businessmen and politicians. Roger was there, having come by horseback with two other ministers: John Cotton and Thomas Hooker.

JOHN WINTHROP WEARILY ARRIVED AT SEMPRINGHAM CASTLE.

As Winthrop entered the room, his disheveled appearance caused many to rise in alarm.

"What on earth has happened to you, Winthrop!" exclaimed Sir Richard Salstonstall, the lord of Ledsham manor.

"The same that has happened to all men on earth. I have fallen, Sir Richard," replied the forty-three-year-old ex-lawyer, brushing his damp curly hair from his narrow, bearded face. "In a bog near Ely on my way. 'Tis the Lord's way of reminding me that only by His grace can I stand clean before Him."

"And 'tis a lesson to the rest of us not to judge a man by his appearance!" laughed Sir Richard.

The humorous exhange put the gathering at ease. Winthrop greeted each man present, and then settled himself into a vacant chair at the head of a long oak table.

"And now, Mr. Hooker," he said, "would you ask the Lord to lead us in our time here together?"

Hooker prayed. "Father of mercies, great and mighty, we beg Thee this day to be among us by Thy Spirit, and to guide Thy poor servants in this vast undertaking.

"We are utterly lost without Thee, and we ask Thee to go

"WHAT ON EARTH HAS HAPPENED TO YOU, WINTHROP!"

before us as Thou went before the Israelites in the wilderness. Show us Thy cloud by day that we may follow Thee. Thy fire by night that we may see Thy presence and know Thy nearness.

"Lead us into Thy Promised Land that we may live by Thy laws only. That we may glorify Thy name, and the name of Thy Holy Son Jesus, among the heathen and to all the nations.

"In all our ways we acknowledge Thee. In all our plans, we trust Thee. Make our paths straight to that New Jerusalem beyond the seas!"

Long into the candlelit night they conferred. With Bibles opened and maps spread out before them, they talked of ships and money, of politics and law, of homes and family. And when all was done, a historic decision had been made: they would buy up the Massachusetts Bay Company—take it over completely—in order to fill Massachusetts with Puritans. They would then begin to build a biblical society, under Winthrop's leadership, in the New World.

The Massachusetts Bay Company was an English colonial enterprise already operating in New England. It had

LONG INTO THE NIGHT THEY CONFERRED.

founded Boston and Salem and a few other small villages in the Massachusetts Bay area. If the Sempringham group could buy the Company, they could help other Puritans to move their families across the sea and build a new order based upon the laws and principles of God's word. Though they didn't plan to separate from the fellowship of the Anglican church, they would still be separated from Old England by the great Atlantic. This would set them free from the persecution of King Charles and Bishop Laud. They could worship God in freedom at last.

As the meeting came to an end, Winthrop's warm, piercing eyes looked around the room at the gathering of tired but excited men. His gaze came to rest upon a large wall tapestry of an old map of England.

"Our nation is heading for disaster," he said with sorrow. "Laud has been transferred to London, where he has begun to shut down Puritan pulpits. He is fast putting out the holy light of the true Gospel."

The candles had burnt low upon the huge table, and Winthrop took one from its holder. He lifted it above his head so that its flame threw a flickering light into the rafters of the

WINTHROP LIFTED THE CANDLE ABOVE HIS HEAD.

high ceiling.

"It may please God to use *us*, in *New* England, to light such a candle that will shine back here from across the sea," he said. "Let us commit ourselves to that purpose, to show our countrymen the way to a more glorious life in God's presence and service. This we shall do in His care and for His Name's sake."

❖

In the spring of 1630, eleven ships, filled with Puritan families, household servants, livestock, and provisions, set sail from Old England toward a new life and a new society over the seas.

Aboard the flagship Arbella—a 350-ton, 38-cannon vessel—John Winthrop delivered a speech that he called "A Model of Christian Charity." He reminded everyone of their calling to this new life together; of the holy society they would be building; of the love and commitment they must have for one another; and of his determination to succeed.

But Roger Williams was not yet a part of this "Great Migration." Back at the Masham estate, he had fallen in love. In December of 1629, he and Mary Barnard had been married

SPRING, 1630
THE GREAT MIGRATION OF PURITANS TO NEW ENGLAND

in the parish church at High Laver, near Otes.

As the Massachussets-bound ships sailed slowly from the shores of Old England, Roger and Mary Williams bade them goodbye. Though Roger's heart was with them, he was not fully at peace about the venture.

"I love those men, Mary," he said one night as the newly-weds sat near the fire in their room at Otes. "Winthrop, especially. Though I don't know him well, I believe he is a great man. His vision is a great vision. And I long to be with him in the wilderness. I long especially to share in the preaching of the Gospel among the natives, for I greatly desire their souls for God. But. . ." And he sighed deeply as he stirred the hot coals with an iron poker.

"But what, my dear?" asked Mary, leaning her head upon his shoulder with her arms around his waist.

"But, what is the sense of crossing the sea and yet remaining part of the Church of England? How can God bless a mission that is tainted by the blood of a Church that wears an earthly Crown, persecutes Christians, and forces the unconverted to sit in its pews?" he replied.

"Perhaps Mr. Winthrop will renounce the Anglican Church

THE NEWLYWEDS SAT BY THE FIRE IN THEIR ROOM AT OTES.

once he is settled in Massachusetts," offered Mary.

"Perhaps," agreed Roger thoughtfully. "He is wise. He is godly. He surely isn't lacking in courage. Perhaps, after passing over the waves and taking up his role as Governor of the colony. . .perhaps."

❖

In December of 1630, Roger travelled to London to visit his aging mother. While he was there, Sydrach pestered him about his Separatist views.

"Separation from the Anglican Church is disobedience to the King," argued Sydrach. "And since the King is God's annointed, given by Heaven to rule our nation, then disobedience to the King is treason against God!"

But Roger was tired of debate with his bitter older brother. "Can't you just let me be what God has made me to be?" Roger pleaded.

"God has nothing to do with what you've become," sneered Sydrach. "You're just a troublemaker and a spiritual snob! And you'll surely get what's coming to you someday."

Roger turned from Sydrach to his mother. "I'll be going now, Mother," he said, as he kissed her on the forehead. "You

"GOD HAS NOTHING TO DO WITH WHAT YOU'VE BECOME!"
SNEERED SYDRACH.

are all in my prayers." With a last pained glance at Sydrach, he headed out the door.

But Sydrach followed him at a distance, and watched as he stopped in to visit his Separatist friends in the home of Derek Baxter.

"The Bishop gave you a warning once, little brother," said Sydrach to the shadows that surrounded him. "I helped you to his attention then, and I believe I'll pay you the honor once again!"

Sydrach, like a Judas, hurried away toward the home of the "High Priest." Laud would be happy to see him.

No sooner had Roger returned to Otes than a messenger from London arrived summoning him to appear before the Bishop on the following day.

"I won't go," Roger told Mary. "If he wants my company so badly, let him come *here* to have tea with me!"

"But you will bring trouble down upon the whole house of Masham," pleaded Mary. "God direct us, what shall we do?"

Roger stared out into the cold November night.

" 'We must stay ahead of the King and his Bishop,' " said

SYDRACH, LIKE A JUDAS, HURRIED TOWARD
THE HOME OF THE "HIGH PRIEST."

Roger. " 'Perhaps we shall sail beyond the horizon.' " He turned to Mary. She ran to his arms and buried her face in his cloak.

Roger continued, "Captain Pierce is back from Massachusetts with his ship, the *Lyon*. He has spent several weeks readying a cargo of supplies to take back to New England. He leaves in two days."

"Do we sail with him, Roger?" asked Mary, looking up into her husband's troubled eyes.

"I believe we must," he replied.

"PERHAPS WE SHALL SAIL BEYOND THE HORIZON."

"SUSANNA, LOOK!" EXCLAIMED MOLLY WINTERS.

7
A.D. 1631-1636
A New England Windmill

"Susannah, look!" exclaimed Molly Winters, dropping her basket of mussels on the beach. She pointed toward the wide horizon where the dark blue waters of Massachusetts Bay met the grey-clouded February sky.

"A ship!" both women shouted, as they gathered up their skirts and ran across the rocks toward the village of Nantasket.

The *Lyon*, with its cargo of twenty passengers and two hundred tons of food, had safely made its way across the storm-tossed ocean. Those aboard were gratefully rejoicing at the sight of land, for they had not felt it beneath their feet in fifty-seven days. Those on land were gratefully rejoicing at the sight of their deliverance, for the colony's food supply was almost gone. A recent proclamation declaring February 6th as a day of humbled fasting was exchanged for a day of thankful feasting. God had answered the colony's prayers twenty-four hours before they were uttered!

Roger and Mary were welcomed to the New World and given a room in the house of Governor Winthrop in Boston.

As the weeks passed, the Williamses became familiar with this "New Jerusalem," and Roger was a guest preacher on Sunday afternoons in the thatched meetinghouse at the head of Boston's only street. To a man who'd been London-born and raised, this rugged little village between the cold sea and the wooded wilderness hardly seemed like either Eden or Jerusalem. But Roger wasn't concerned about either comfort or culture. His heart burned with a passion for biblical Christianity and a purified Church, concerns that overshadowed his present primitive surroundings.

In March, John Wilson, pastor of the Boston Church, announced that he was returning to England to fetch his wife back to Massachusetts. Wilson suggested to the Governor and the colony's ruling Magistrates that Roger Williams take his place in the pulpit during his absense. The Magistrates unanimously agreed, and they formally offered Roger the honored post.

But Roger turned them down. Boston was astounded.

"What is your reason for refusing this pulpit, Master Rogers?" asked Winthrop, as he and Roger sat together in Winthrop's study.

BOSTON WAS A RUGGED LITTLE VILLAGE BETWEEN THE COLD
SEA AND THE WOODED WILDERNESS.

ROGER WILLIAMS

"I dare not give communion to an unseparated people," Roger bluntly said. "As long as Boston still holds the hand of the English Church, she touches the robes of Antichrist."

"Antichrist! Williams, the Anglican Church may be less than pure, but she is Protestant! And there are many godly men and women within her fellowship," countered Winthrop.

"The Anglican Church is a false church," argued Roger. "Her roots don't reach to the Apostles. They are tangled in the rocky soil of the Roman Catholic Apostacy, and they suck their poisoned doctrines from the council chambers of the King.

"We must 'come out from among them,' as the Apostle Paul commands us," Roger insisted. "We must repent, and separate ourselves from the English Church completely, if we are ever to recover the lost Zion."

"Did your ocean journey upset your senses as well as your stomach, Williams? This colony *depends* on our company charter from the King. If we loose ourselves from the Anglican Church, we risk the loss of our right to exist! Should we tempt the Lord by cutting off the branch while we sit on it? Though I mourn the corruption of our mother church, still I believe she has the nature of the Truth in her," reasoned

"SHOULD WE TEMPT THE LORD BY CUTTING OFF THE BRANCH WHILE WE SIT ON IT?"

Winthrop.

But Roger could not be convinced, and at last he bid the Governor good night.

Winthrop sat alone in his darkened study, puzzled by this godly young zealot who had begun to trouble the waters of the Massachusetts Bay Colony.

Weeks turned into months, and the men of Boston—Williams and Winthrop included—rolled up their sleeves in the common work of thicket-clearing, wall-raising, wood-gathering, and fence-building. Hay was gathered on nearby islands. Framed, thatched cottages began to replace the many wigwams and tents of the Puritan planters. But before spring arrived or anyone had yet prepared a garden or a crop, Roger was sowing more seeds of discontent. In his commitment to proclaim the truth as he saw it, he didn't seem to realize that he was tugging at the rug upon which his friends and neighbors stood.

This time he challenged the Magistrates' right to punish Sabbath-breaking.

The Magistrates were the colony's law makers and policemen. Committed to the Puritan vision of a community built upon biblical laws and morality, they firmly believed

RAISING WALLS AND BUILDING FENCES

that God would bless them and dwell among them only as the community sought to obey Him. In The Massachusetts Bay Colony, the Puritans were Congregationalist. That meant that members of each Church congregation chose their own pastors and ran their own affairs. They also elected the Magistrates and the Governor that would oversee the business of colonial government. This was very different from the English Church where all congregations were ruled by Ministers appointed by the Bishop, and the Bishop himself was appointed by the King. However, though the Bay churches were glad their English King was far across the waters, they still believed that government must enforce the laws of both the State and the Church.

The foundational laws of the Bay were the Ten Commandments that God had given to Moses. There were no higher laws known to man, and so upon these Commandments, the Magistrates laid the stones of their New Jerusalem.

To insure that the people lived, and hopefully believed, according to God's principles, everyone was required to go to church on Sundays (once in the morning and once in the afternoon) and on certain other days of the week. The commandment to "honor the Sabbath and keep it holy" was strictly

"REMEMBER THE SABBATH DAY TO KEEP IT HOLY."

enforced, and no one was allowed to work or travel (except to church) on Sunday. Those who "broke the Sabbath" were sometimes fined, sometimes publicly admonished, whipped or placed in the stocks. The nature of their Sabbath-breaking determined the type of punishment. The law for Sunday church attendance was also a law in England at the time, and most folks didn't think it a strange requirement for life in a land that acknowledged God and his Son, Jesus Christ.

But not all folks think alike.

"The Apostle Paul tells us that each man may keep his own Sabbath. It is a matter of conscience between an individual and God," Roger reasoned. "And if a man is not a Christian, how can we force him to honor the Sabbath at all?"

The Magistrates disagreed. "If we allow everyone to do as he pleases, our colony will fall apart at the seams. We have convenanted to submit ourselves to God and to our leaders," they said. "We cannot build a holy society if we let unholiness and disorder run loose in the streets."

Roger believed there must be punishment for those who break God's laws in regard to relationships and property, but he argued that the laws of the First Table (the first four of the Ten Commandments) were matters between each person and

A "SABBATH BREAKER" IN THE STOCKS

God alone. Roger's contentions were threatening the authority of the men responsible for peace and order in the colony. Couldn't he see that he was digging a pit for them all to fall into?

But Roger couldn't see it, and so he kept on digging. Meanwhile, the Magistrates could not agree on what to do about the man. Apart from his strange opinions, they respected and admired him. He was a good and honest neighbor, a gifted preacher, and an unselfish, compassionate, and hard working member of the community. Perhaps he would see the errors of his way.

In April of that year, the nearby town of Salem invited Roger to assist their ailing pastor Samuel Skelton, and to be Teacher in the place of their former pastor John Higginson (who had died the preceding summer). Believing Salem to be more Separatist at heart, Roger accepted. But Winthrop was worried that this young firebrand would cause too much trouble if given a pulpit from which to spread his weird philosophies. The Assistants (the Governor's Council) strongly advised the Salem congregation to think twice before installing Roger Williams as their new pastor. But Salem had already made its decision.

ROGER WAS A GOOD NEIGHBOR.

ROGER WILLIAMS

Roger and Mary moved to Salem, and Roger assumed the pulpit. But his rigidly Separatist views proved too strong for Salem as well, and it wasn't long before the Williamses chose to pack up their belongings again. This time they sailed twenty-five miles south, out of Puritan jurisdiction and into strictly Separatist territory. Their destination: Plymouth.

❖

Roger became a Pilgrim.

The hillside settlement of Plymouth had been born out of a Separatist congregation that moved from England to Holland in 1608 to escape persecution. In 1620, it pulled up roots again, sailing for the New World in a small ship called *The Mayflower*. The Plymouth colony was older and larger than either Boston or Salem. It was more prosperous as well, and allowed its citizens a bit more freedom, but it was beginning to wane in its spiritual fervor and mission. Roger sensed the spiritual laxity, and rose to the occasion, assisting pastor Ralph Smith in the care of the souls of Plymouth.

Meanwhile, he hoed his acre of land and planted his corn. He purchased cattle from Boston through Winthrop. He learned the Dutch language from his neighbors who had lived in Holland.

ROGER BECAME A PILGRIM.

ROGER WILLIAMS

And he made many new friends. There was the cheerful patriarch and Elder, William Brewster, with his library of four-hundred books. There was the prudent and godly Governor, William Bradford, who had recently turned—in his spare time—to the study of Hebrew and to the writing of poetry and a *History of Plymouth Plantation.* There was the fiery little soldier and guardian of Plymouth, Captain Miles Standish. There was the softhearted Pilgrim deacon, psalm-singer, and physician, Samuell Fuller. And there was the ex-printer, merchant, and Indian expert, Edward Winslow. It was Winslow who led Roger into the woods one day to meet a man who would change Roger's life.

The sunlight filtered through the tall oaks, highlighting patches of gold and green upon the thickly ferned forest floor. Birds flew and deer fled as Edward and Roger slid past moss-covered rocks and over the giant rotted skeleton of an ancient spruce. The path they were following was a slim, well-worn trail that wound through the tall trees toward a village of the Narragansett Indians.

As they came out of the woods into a clearing beside a flowing stream, they spotted a dark-skinned Native washing

THE TRAIL WOUND THROUGH THE TREES TOWARD A VILLAGE
OF THE NARRAGANSETT INDIANS.

his hands and face at the edge of the water.

"What cheer, Nétop (friend)?" Edward shouted to the man.

"Asco wequassunnúmmis (good morning), Nétop!" returned the tall, thin Indian. "What brings you to our country, Winslow?"

"I am here to see Canonicus, Wassáppi," replied Edward. "He is expecting us. I have brought a friend who wishes to meet him."

Wassáppi guided the two Englishmen into the village and to the door of the house of the Grand Sachem, Canonicus. The Sachem's dwelling was a long building of poles, covered over with mats made of animal hides. It had three fires inside, and three fire holes in its ceiling. Its inside walls were decorated with colorfully embroidered mats made by the women of the village.

"Come in, Winslow," said the aged Sachem. "Come in and sit down."

Edward and Roger entered the smokey dwelling, and for a moment Roger could hardly breath.

Canonicus remained seated and motioned for them to recline. When they had done so, the great chief spread his arms out to them in greeting, and smiled.

"COME IN AND SIT DOWN," SAID THE AGED SACHEM.

ROGER WILLIAMS

Prince over the nation of the Narragansetts—by far the largest and most powerful tribe in New England—Canonicus had ruled for many decades. Though seventy years of age, the Sachem still had his health and his wits. The English feared him for the authority he held, but they respected him for his wisdom and his genuine desire to live at peace with them. He, in his turn, respected the English for their superior inventions, their powerful weapons, and their great ships. He was wise enough to see that the ships kept coming. "Perhaps," he thought, "they will always come. If so, I must lead my people to stand firmly on our land, but always at peace when peace is offered." Though he was puzzled that Manìt (the Narragansett God) had allowed the English to come into his land, he was not afraid of what each day held. But he felt that the God of the English must be more powerful than the God of the Indians, because He had given the English books and clothes and many other marvelous things.

In fact, God was the subject of this day's conversation, and the reason for Roger's first visit to the house of Canonicus.

"I am Canonicus," said the old Sachem to the young Pilgrim. "You are Roger Williams. You wish to talk about God. We will talk about God."

PRINCE OF THE NARRAGANSETTS,
CANONICUS HAD RULED FOR MANY DECADES.

And for the next three hours, the Indian King and the English Preacher talked religion. In that short time, on that sunny summer morning, their two hearts were strangely united in a bond of affection and respect that would grow stronger and truer in the years ahead. As the time came for Roger and Edward to depart, Canonicus made one last comment concerning their discussion:

"You have shown me the Book which God Himself made, concerning men's souls. I cannot read its writings as you can. So perhaps you know more than I do about these things. Still, I must trust in my forefathers, for they received their knowledge from God as well."

"There is one God and one Truth," replied Roger. "Just as there is one Canonicus. If another of your people should claim to be Canonicus and should declare things in your name, yet he is not Canonicus, and his words are not yours. Whoever follows him would be following a false Sachem."

Canonicus nodded thoughtfully. "We will talk more of these matters on another day," he said.

❖

As the seasons came and went, Roger spent more and more time among the Indians. With Winslow's help, he set up a

"THERE IS ONE GOD AND ONE TRUTH," SAID ROGER.

trading business with them, and contacted his brother Robert in England to arrange for shipments of goods to Plymouth. He learned the Narragansett language and customs, and preached to them at all opportunities. He met Sachems of other tribes. He slept in their smokey tents. He ate with them around their fires. And as his heart was more and more inclined toward their souls, he wrote to Winthrop that he would like to be a missionary among them. During this time of concourse with the Natives, he formed some ideas that would get him into more trouble than he had yet known in this new world.

"Mary, I'm beginning to believe that the land upon which the English stand is sinfully won," said Roger one evening as he warmed his feet by the fire of his hearth.

Mary urged him on with a surprised nod, as she stirred the soup that hung over the flames.

Roger continued, "This land was the Natives' before we came. Before the English or the Dutch or the French. The Indians settled it and farmed it and hunted it for generations that only God knows of. And yet with one planting of the English flag on its soil, the King declares it his. Then he gives it to whomever he wills, but with no consideration of

ROGER LEARNED THE NARRAGANSETT
LANGUAGE AND CUSTOMS.

its Native population."

"Roger, it belongs to England by right of discovery. And we have it from the King's hand as a gift from God," replied Mary, puzzled by her husband's latest revelations.

"Discovery? It was already discovered, and indeed inhabited, by the savages who have lived upon it for years. And they consider it a gift from God as well, though they know Him not," said Roger. "I have thought about this much, and have been writing about it whenever I have a moment to spare. I mean to share my thoughts with Governor Bradford if ever I find the time."

"God will make the time when He has the set the purpose, dear Roger," said Mary with resignation. "But, here, the soup is ready."

After a prayer of thanksgiving and blessing for God's provision, Roger and Mary quietly ate their supper. Mary kept her eyes on the man she loved, as he sat in silent thought. She waited for him to come out of his dreaming, in order to tell him something that had been upon her heart all day. But he seemed to be so far away this night, and he didn't speak again until the meal had ended.

"Thank you," he said suddenly, looking up at Mary with a

ROGER AND MARY QUIETLY ATE THEIR SUPPER.

warm smile. "The soup was delicious. I am full and satisfied."

Mary pulled her chair closer to his, and reached out to hold his calloused hands.

"Roger," she said, with a gentle glimmer in her eyes.

"Yes, dearest," he replied, returning her gaze with a tired but attentive sigh.

"Roger," she said again. "You are going to be a father."

❖

In June of 1633, only two months before Mary was due to have her baby, Roger received a message from Salem. Samuel Skelton, like his predecessor at Salem, was slowly dying of tuberculosis. Though Salem had chafed at the preaching of Williams only two years earlier, it was in desperate need of someone to assume the burden of five services a week. Knowing Roger was a committed and gifted teacher, the congregation called upon him once again.

Out of pity for his dying friend, and believing it to be a temporary charge, Roger returned to Salem. He was thirty years old.

In August, little Mary Williams was born. But with the joys of parenthood came the responsibilities of the same. As

"ROGER, YOU ARE GOING TO BE A FATHER."

Skelton grew less able to lead, Roger was soon saddled with the main care of the Salem church. Added to Roger's load was his continued trade and preaching among the Indians, along with the farming of his land. His days were hard and long, and they left Roger wearied and weakened.

Still, he pressed on, and under his preaching, the Salem congregation experienced a deep conviction of sin and a revived spiritual life in God. Under the influence of Roger's zeal and eloquence, moved by his warmheartedness and his sterling character, Salem took on the image of its new spiritual leader. Much to the dismay of the rest of the colony, the town became a stronghold of radical Separatism.

On top of it all, while still in Plymouth, Roger had managed to finish his little treatise on land rights. Winthrop had recently heard of it through Bradford, and he was much disturbed. He asked Roger for a copy, and when he had read it, he shared it with his Assistants. After digesting the unsettling contents of the pamphlet, which basically disputed the right of Massachusetts and New Plymouth to their land, the Assistants summoned Roger.

In Boston, in March of 1634, Roger stood before the Governor and his Court.

ROGER PREACHED REPENTANCE AND REVIVAL.

"Master Williams," said Winthrop. "If God wasn't pleased in giving us this land, why did He drive out the Natives before us? Why does He still make room for us by sending the smallpox among the savages, diminishing them that we may increase? Why has He planted his churches here?"

"Sir," replied Roger humbly, "I must admit that God has slain many of the Natives by His own hand, and that we are here in their stead. But it is beyond my understanding."

Winthrop continued, "Even if we had no right to this land, God has full right to it. And if He is pleased to give it to us, taking it from a people who have so long usurped Him, who shall argue with Him?"

"I shall not," replied Roger. "But neither shall I claim the land as mine unless I pay for it out of my own pocketbook. The King, though he call this land his own, has no more right to give it away than Canonicus has the right to give London away to the Narragansetts."

"How can you say this?" asked Winthrop. "I agree with you that as a colony we must deal as Christians with the savages. But the right of discovery is international law! And to speak against the King will only provoke him against us. If you truly loved the peace of our churches in New England,

"HOW CAN YOU SAY THIS?" ASKED WINTHROP.

you would not so rashly put a sword in the King's hand to destroy us!"

Roger felt the sting, and indeed the truth, of Winthrop's words. Though he fully believed the logic of his own arguments, he could not deny the logic of the Court. Looking around at the judicial gathering, he apologized for the anguish and concern his book had caused them.

"I meant it only to be a sharing of my private thoughts with Governor Bradford," Roger explained. "I am sorry it has drug us all to Court and to controversy. You may burn it, or any part of it, for all I care."

But Roger did not remain penitent for long. His love for the Natives, his hatred for the "anti-Christian" Church of England, and his passion for truth as he saw it, overpowered the sensible reasonings of Governor Winthrop. He resumed his preaching against the King's right to give away land in New England, and he condemned the sinfulness of those who accepted it from the King. He even wrote a letter to Charles, accusing him of various sins against God, and admonishing him to repent.

Meanwhile, news had arrived from England that Charles was planning to revoke the Bay Company's charter and to

ROGER WROTE A LETTER TO KING CHARLES.

appoint a Royal Governor in New England. And Laud, with the King's permission, was threatening to impose Anglican discipline upon the colony. In fact, a ship had been built especially to carry the new Governor to the New World.

But God, with His eye out for the redeemed of New England (and for reasons that were surely His own alone), headed the King off at the pass. While the new ship was being launched, it split in half and sank.

Divine intervention or not, Roger could not have picked a worse time to be railing against the King or the Anglican Church. But truth was truth to him. Let the heads fall where they may!

The final straw in his attack on Bay authority came in his opposition to their *Oath of Fidelity* and their request for a standard church discipline for all the Bay congregations.

Roger spoke out against this unified church discipline, and against the Magistrates' right to enforce it, because he felt that it struck at the heart of an independent congregation's right to run its own race under God. The Magistrates understood his logic, but they were getting tired of his repeated attacks against their authority. Didn't he know that these were dangerous times and that a stronger hand was needed at the

THE NEW SHIP SPLIT IN HALF AND SANK.

helm of government? They didn't want to take away free-doms, they wanted to insure them for the future by pulling things together during this time of crisis.

The *Oath* was an attempt by the Magistrates to insure the loyalty of Bay residents against the threat of Charles and his Royal Governor. Since many strangers had recently arrived in the Bay with no intent to settle in the colony, the Magistrates needed a way to make them promise to abide by the laws of the land while they were living there. Surely Roger could see the need for that.

But Roger's eyes were clouded. Perhaps it was the incredible daily load he labored under. Perhaps it was the tearing away from one civilized, all-familiar world to the wild, blank slate of another. Perhaps it was the sickness that he now endured, that kept him under the care of two physicians (but rarely kept him from his duties). Perhaps it was the constant tension between him and the Bay, a tension strained to the breaking point by continual callings before the Court of Assistants. Perhaps it was simply the pride and passion of a youthful idealism that carried his biblical conscience above the practical realities of maintaining a stable government in the wilderness. Whatever it was that drove Roger to declare

BUT ROGER'S EYES WERE CLOUDED.

his personal position at all points, he spoke out against the *Oath* with apparently no recognition of the problem the Magistrates were trying to meet. His words, too often, gave others reason to rebel against the government.

His own reason, as always, was not political, but spiritual.

"We must never ask an unsaved man to take an oath before God. An oath is something between a man's conscience and the Almighty," argued Roger. "Besides, the Lord Jesus said that no man should swear an oath. We are to say 'Yes' or 'No' to all that is asked of us. Anything else, scripture declares, is from the evil one."

The Magistrates, the Bay ministers, the Governor and his Assistants, indeed most anyone in the Bay, would gladly have entered a discussion on the words of Jesus. They did so each Sunday in order to better understand the commands and the ways of God. They did so as they went about their days: fishing, hunting, farming, building, trading, eating, drinking, playing. But this Cyclone from Salem was blowing up a storm that far exceeded the gentle winds of doctrinal debate. This storm must be stilled or the authority of the Magistrates would be brought to nothing and the Bay would be thrown into civil dissension. A house divided cannot stand.

"A HOUSE DIVIDED CANNOT STAND."

ROGER WILLIAMS

"Was Williams this much of a radical back in Old England," asked newly elected Governor John Haynes to a special gathering of Bay ministers one chilly October day in 1635.

Haynes had arrived in New England, along with Roger's old friends John Cotton and Thomas Hooker, in September of 1633. Hooker became Pastor at Newtown, and Cotton accepted the Boston pulpit which Roger had refused. Haynes had beat out Winthrop in a recent election for the governorship.

"Perhaps he was, and simply didn't declare it as loudly or as often," answered Cotton. "But in coming here he has discovered himself."

Haynes did not know Roger as Winthrop did. He had no special affection for him or appreciation for his better qualities. He only saw Williams as a troublemaker whose trouble must be ended, one way or another, immediately.

On October 8, Roger—though sick—came once more to Court. It was no ordinary assembly that was gathered at the Newtown Church for the General Court session. Besides all the Ministers in the Bay, the Magistrates and the Assistants were also present. Governor Haynes presided.

"Master Williams," said Hooker, who had been chosen to

"WAS WILLIAMS THIS MUCH OF A RADICAL BACK IN OLD ENGLAND?" ASKED GOVERNOR HAYNES.

convince Roger of the error of his actions and opinions. "Will you not cease in your digging of ditches beneath our Churches? Will you not hear the arguments of your brothers and colleagues? Will you not bow before God in the matter of obedience to the civil authorities of the Bay?"

"I bow before God daily, Thomas," answered Roger. "My life and breath, what there is of both, are His alone. My allegience is His alone."

"What of Paul's words to the Romans that whoever resists the power of the civil authorities is therefore resisting the ordinances of God?" questioned Hooker.

Roger was stunned. How often had he heard that argument from the lips of English Kings and Bishops? Heard it used to shame good Church folk into mindless submission. How often had they all heard it? And hadn't they crossed the seas—Hooker included—to escape the persecution of men who claimed a special right to divine authority? Roger simply shook his fever-flushed face in disbelief and posed a question of his own.

"Do not the civil authorities of the Bay, whom I respect for men of godliness and faithfulness, also need to bow before God? My arguments against them are not against their

HADN'T THEY CROSSED THE SEAS TO ESCAPE PERSECUTION?

authority, but against an un-Christian use of it."

Hooker quickly retorted, "Then you hold to all that you have spoken against them? To all that you have written? To all that you have done to tear down what they would build?"

Roger's reddened eyes flashed with conviction and pain. Not conviction of any sin of his own, unfortunately, but of the rightness of his opinions. Not with pain for the men who had patiently endured his attacks, but for their misunderstanding his heart. Pride blinded him to their own love for him, and to their own undeniable sacrifices for the truth. If Roger had any more light than they did, he did not yet have the wisdom to simply lift up a candle in the darkness as Winthrop had done those years before at Sempringham.

"I hold to it all," said Roger, as he looked from face to face around the room, "as I would to any doctrine of the Lord Jesus upon which you or I would gladly give our lives. But if I am guilty of tearing anything down, it is only because my heart burns for a Heavenly City not made by hands, whose pattern we must strive to follow in all that we do!"

"I have no further questions, Governor," said Hooker sadly as he turned the proceedings back over to Haynes.

Two days later, Roger and the Court met again. As Roger

"I HOLD TO IT ALL," SAID ROGER.

stood, Haynes read the Court's sentence. Much of it seemed a dream to Roger, but the final words struck him with the force of a charging horse.

"...whereas Roger Williams has introduced and divulged various new and dangerous opinions against the authority of Magistrates, and yet maintains these opinions without retracting them, he must depart from the Massachusetts Bay Colony within six weeks. If he fails to heed this order of expulsion, the Magistrates have full authority to send him to some place out of this jurisdicition."

Banished! A man twice without a country. This was not just a dream, it was a nightmare.

But Roger was not a man given to despair.

That same month, Mary gave birth to her second child. They named the girl *Freeborn*.

"Mary, Mary," moaned Roger as he lay upon his sickbed in Salem. "Bring me water, dear! I'm so thirsty."

Mary lifted a pewter cup to his hot lips. "Drink, and then sleep, darling," she whispered, as he lay back upon the piled pillows.

"I dreamed that I saw the Bride of Christ, coming down

BANISHED!

out of Heaven. Beautiful, she was, strong and pure and full of life," mumbled Roger with his eyes closed. "When will that day come? Why must these days be so full of stumbling and confusion?"

"Sleep, darling," Mary repeated, as she wiped the silent tears from her own eyes. "Sleep, and dream of heaven."

"He always dream of heaven, whether he sleep or not," said a tall and powerful Indian who was standing beside the bed.

"Yes, you're right, Miantonomy," Mary smiled, "And that is why I love him."

"I love him, too," said the Sachem, "But not because he dream of Heaven. I love him for his love for me and for my Uncle Canonicus. I love him for his truth-speaking and his courage. Roger know God. God know Roger. God make him well again. Many things for him to do. Many people need him."

Mary touched the dark-skinned arm in thanks for Miantonomy's sincere words. She looked with awed appreciation into his wild eyes, and then she left the room. Late that night Roger awakened briefly. In the darkness of his bedchamber, he could see the silhouetted form of a swarthy

"SLEEP, DARLING, AND DREAM OF HEAVEN."

"guardian angel," kneeling in perfect stillness beside the bed. Miantonomy was keeping watch, perhaps praying silently on Roger's behalf to the radical preacher's Jesus.

❖

Six weeks came and went. The Bay knew that Roger was ill, and so they didn't press for his immediate removal. In fact, they gave him until next spring, provided he not try to draw others into agreement with his opinions. But as the weeks turned to months, they began to hear rumors that he was planning to start a colony around Narragansett Bay. They heard that twenty people were interested in joining him. Whether this was true or not, they could no longer afford to have this New England Windmill grind out grain for bread that would poison their people.

They decided they must send him back to England, and a small ship was hired, under the command of Captain Underhill, to sail around to Salem and pack him off over the seas.

But Roger had many friends in high places, and someone got the news to him before Underhill could carry out his orders. It was January of 1636, and the winter had been an incredibly wild and snowy one. When the Captain finally

MIANTONOMY WAS KEEPING WATCH.

hove into icy Salem harbor and trudged through the snow to knock on the door of the Williams' house, Roger had been gone three days.

ROGER HAD BEEN GONE THREE DAYS.

ROGER FORCED HIMSELF THROUGH THE WHITE WILDERNESS.

8
A.D. 1636
Another Winter Day

Even among the pines and under the tallest trees, the snow lay heavy. At woods-edge and along frozen streams, it was drifted high. Rivers were hardened avenues of ice and crusted snow, and the frigid wind blew hard through the leafless forest. On this second day of Roger's wearied flight, a freezing rain fell with such sharpness that it threatened to cut the very bark from off the trees.

Fighting the bone-chilling cold and the feelings of despair and lostness that flew at him with each new wind-driven blast of winter rain, Roger forced himself through the white wilderness into the heart of the Wampanoag Country.

Though he well knew the way in fair weather, the landscape had been transformed by long and bitter months of hail and snow from Heaven. It was only by the most obvious landmarks that Roger kept himself on the trail that he was following. But even now, his feverish mind was fighting to reach beyond this cold external world to a reality that transcended

Nature's times and seasons.

" 'Though your sins be as scarlet, they shall be white as snow,' " Roger quoted to himself. "Where is my sin in standing for Truth, Lord God? What is this cleansing that drives me from my hearth and home, from my wife and children? Where is the fellowship of the brethren and the love of God in this vast, white Hell? If I live, I shall feel these moments 'til the day I die!"

Beside him, valiantly struggling through drifts that would frustrate a giant, was Roger's young domestic servant, Thomas Angell. Together, the thirty-three-year-old refugee and his fifteen-year-old servant slowly plowed a sixty-mile trail that Nature quickly closed behind them. At this frozen moment in time, Roger couldn't possibly know the long trail that God had marked out for him to walk in the decades ahead. He had no inkling of his fuller destiny or calling. No desire whatever to be written into any chapters of anyone's history. No thoughts of tomorrow. As he stumbled desperately through the drifting landscape, he had only one thing in mind: the shelter of the tents of the Wampanoag Indians.

As they crossed the flat meadow country of the

THEY STUMBLED DESPERATELY
THROUGH THE DRIFTING LANDSCAPE.

Wampanoags, the smoke from the wigwams of the town of Sowams came finally into view. Numbly, the ice-covered Englishmen staggered into the startled village. Barely able to return the greetings of the Natives who met them, they were ushered to the home of the Sachem, Massasoit. There, next to the fire of the Wampanoag Chieftain, they fell in exhausted thankfulness upon the smoky mats, and slept.

*IN EXHAUSTED THANKFULNESS,
UPON THE SMOKEY MATS THEY SLEPT.*

WITHIN THE WARM TENTS OF THE WAMPANOAGS...

9
A.D. 1636
Providence

Within the warm tents of the Wampanoags, Roger was nursed to health. The youthful strength that had failed him during his time and ministry among his own, now returned in the quiet winter days among the Indians. He spoke often with them of God and His Son, but he never once confessed the reason for his strange sojourn through the bitter January storm. He sent word to Mary that he was well, and that he would send for her soon. He also counselled long with Massasoit, and the two of them spoke of Roger's desire to settle near the Seekonk River on land that he had bought from Massasoit several years earlier.

"You bring your family there," said the Sachem. "And some of your countrymen. You build your houses and plant your corn. And we will trade. We will be friends, Williams. I trust you. You speak true."

"If you need my help, I'll give it," said Roger. "If you need food and goods, I'll trade with you for them. If you wish to know the True God, I'll teach you and your sons and daughers about Him. And I'll live among you in peace, as God desires that we must."

When Roger was finally well enough to travel again, he and Angell crossed over the border into the Narragansett Country to visit with Canonicus.

"You are coming to live among us at last!" exclaimed the aged Sachem. "I am happy to see this day, for I love you as a son. You are more than English, Roger. You are like one who comes to all men as a friend. When you tell me of Jesus, I can think of no man like Him but you."

"I am honored that you would call me a son, Canonicus," said Roger, humbled and warmed at heart. He thought longingly of his own father and of Sir Edward Coke. "But I am not at all like the Savior. He is pure and righteous, I am full of sin."

"I am full of sin, too, my son," said the great Chief. "My heart is one big stone. I pray to Manìt, and to your God's Son Jesus, that they will take my sin away. But perhaps my sin is stronger than yours, stronger even than the power of your Christ, because still it is within me. It always rises to darken

"I AM FULL OF SIN, TOO, MY SON."

my eyes."

"If we say we have no sin, we are liars, says God's book. But if we confess our sins, He is faithful and just to forgive us our sins," admonished Roger.

"What more does God want from me, Roger?" asked Canonicus sincerely.

"To turn from all the idols in your heart, in your worship, and in your life. And to trust in Christ Jesus alone. Then you will be able to worship the True and Living God," Roger replied.

❖

Just before spring, Roger and Angell set out for the eastern shore of the Seekonk, to the spot that Roger and Massasoit had marked out years before. Here, the two companions raised a simple shelter and began to lay crops in the fertile ground. Here also they were joined by three men from Salem: a poor and destitute attorney's clerk named William Harris, a miller from Dorchester (also banished) named John Smith, and a poor young fellow named Francis Wicks. Though Roger desired a more hermitlike existence among the Indians, his heart was moved by these desperate men who had invited

THE TWO COMPANIONS RAISED A SIMPLE SHELTER.

themselves to settle with him. He told them they could stay.

By now, the Bay had heard that Roger was alive. Good friends were much relieved, and most who wished him gone still wished him well. But what many wished even more was that he was a wee bit further away. Though Roger was on land he had purchased from Massasoit, he was also still within the jurisdiction of Plymouth. Roger's old friend Edward Winslow (now Governor of Plymouth), not wanting any trouble with the Bay, sent a messenger advising Roger simply to cross to the other side of the river so that he and Plymouth could freely live as loving neighbors. So Roger and his company left their half-planted crops in ground that Roger had bought for his own, and set their sights for the western shores of the Seekonk.

❖

A slender canoe slipped down the wide river as the mid-April sun danced upon the ripples caused by the dipping, sliding oars. Along the shore line, a huddle of Indians watched the five men slowly rowing. As the canoe came nearer, the leader of the white men shouted, "What cheer, Netop?" and he motioned to the Natives that he would be landing on the neck of

A HUDDLE OF INDIANS WATCHED THE MEN SLOWLY ROWING.

ground just around the bend. The band of Indians followed as the canoe continued toward its destination.

At an outcropping of slate, Roger guided the boat into land. As he stood up in the front of the canoe to lay hold onto the rock, an Indian extended his hand. Red hand and white hand embraced in a clasp of friendship and greeting as Roger stepped onto the shore.

He smiled at the savages gathered curiously around him, then stared up into the azure spring sky.

"By God's mercy and providence, He has been with me in my distress," confessed Roger aloud. "I sense His Presence in this place. Should Canonicus sell me land on these shores, I shall call this place Providence."

RED HAND AND WHITE HAND EMBRACED IN FRIENDSHIP.

WINTHROP CLOSED THE INSIDE SHUTTERS
OF HIS STUDY WINDOW.

10
A.D. 1636
Blessed are the Peacemakers

Winthrop closed the inside shutters of his study window, turned the wick up higher in his lamp, and sat down at his desk. An election in May (that had won Sir Henry Vane the Massachusetts Governorship over John Haynes) had restored Winthrop to power by giving him the seat of second-in-command. Now, as Deputy Governor, he had an urgent message to pen. Taking out his ink and sharpening his quill, he pulled a sheet of parchment from his desk drawer. A small stack of letters within the drawer caught his attention, and he took them out. They were letters from Roger, written from Providence over the past several months. Winthrop opened the first one he had received:

". . .it was not price or money that purchased Providence. 'Tis true Canonicus received many presents and gifts from me, but neither a thousand nor ten thousand dollars could have bought from him an English entrance into his land. He is very wary of the English, though not in the least afraid of us. No amount of money could have bought Providence, or any other land I have from him. Providence was purchased by love."

"May that love, and indeed the providence of God, serve us in this dark hour!" said Winthrop.

He opened another letter:

". . .it is not true that I was hired by any, or made covenant with any, or desired that anyone come with me into this wilderness. But they have come, and I have yielded to their interest to settle here. I have rented out portions of my land to those who will have it, and I have ordered that no man be molested for his conscience. If nowhere else, men may come to Providence and be free."

"Roger, dear Roger, your soft heart will call down trouble upon your hard head! For soon every heretic and moral rebel will be knocking at your door," Winthrop commented. "But we must *lock* our doors and take up arms if we are to be truly free in these frightful days."

Then he slipped Roger's latest letter from its envelope. It was dated October 7, 1636. Yesterday.

". . .the Pequot Indians, seemingly as evil as their father

THEN WINTHROP READ ROGER'S LATEST LETTER.

Satan, have determined to annihilate the English. Only days ago they attacked and murdered several of our countrymen outside Saybrook Fort on the Connecticut River. The war between the Pequots and the Narragansetts being at an end, and peace now promised between the two, the Pequots have sent ambassadors to Miantonomy. They wish to form an alliance with the Sachem and his Uncle against the English, to push us back into the sea. I pray God will have mercy upon us and frustrate all their counsels."

"May God have mercy indeed, friend Williams!" said Winthrop with resolve. "And may He use *you*, and your bond of love with the Narragansett Chiefs, to do the frustrating!"

The Deputy set the letters to one side, dipped his quill into the inkpot, and began to write:

"Dear Roger,

"On behalf of the Governor of Massachusetts and his Assistants, I am asking you to put your life into God's hand in an errand of the utmost import. . ."

When Roger received the message from Winthrop, he did not hesitate. Scarcely acquainting his wife with his desperate

". . .THEY ATTACKED OUR COUNTRYMEN."

assignment, he set off immediately. . .and alone. A hazard-
ous thirty-mile voyage over troubled waters would take him
to his destination: the great wigwam city of Canonicus.

The dark waters of the Narragansett Bay danced violently
to the shrill song of the howling fall wind. Roger plowed
through the cold, salty waves, forcing his oar through the
water on one side of his canoe and then on the other. The
little boat rose and fell like a ship on a tempest-tossed sea.
As the long hours passed and the city of the great Sachem
finally came into view, Roger cried out in weary thanks for
God's protection, and prayed for His help in the task ahead.
When Roger hove up on the shores of Canonicus's capitol,
the hand of God was as strong upon him as the heavy surf
that had soaked him to the skin.

The sight of this storm-blasted Englishman, striding tall
and full of purpose, caused many of the Natives to shrink
back as Roger entered the packed State-house where the con-
niving Pequots were parleying with Canonicus and
Miantonomy.

"What this English doing here?" demanded the head
Pequot ambassador.

ROGER PLOWED THROUGH THE COLD, SALTY WAVES.

"Why not ask him, yourself," said Miantonomy gravely. But Canonicus simply motioned for Roger to take a seat near the fire.

"We are talking of a pact together," the Grand Sachem said to Roger. "One which would unite our peoples against any further trespassing of the English. And of course, that is why you have come, is it not?"

"That is why I have come," Roger replied.

For three days and nights Roger lodged with the Indians, counselling with Canonicus, reasoning with Miantonomy, arguing against the appeals of the Pequots, and pleading instead for an alliance between the English and the Narragansetts. All the while, he imagined he could smell the blood of his countrymen upon the hands and arms of the Pequot ambassadors. Nightly, he expected them to put a knife to his throat. But God wondrously protected him and helped him at last to shatter the Pequot's plans. Miantonomy was quickly won to Roger's cause, but Canonicus was a harder case.

"I have never decreed any wrong be done to the English since he landed," declared Canonicus. "And as long as the

ROGER PLEADED FOR AN ALLIANCE
BETWEEN THE ENGLISH AND THE NARRAGANSETTS.

Englishman speaks true, then I shall go to my grave in peace. But if he speaks lies, if he takes what belongs to me and my people, I will not stand aside. I will do all I can to stop him."

"But you have no cause to question the Englishman's faithfulness," replied Roger. "You have had long experience of his friendliness and trustiness." Though some English, as well as French and Dutch, had treated the Indians unfairly, even treacherously, Roger knew that the Bay had always pursued a Christian policy of peace and respect toward its Indian neighbors.

Canonicus picked up a stick near the fire, and broke it in ten pieces. He then related ten instances (laying down a piece of stick with each instance) that gave him cause to doubt the Englishman's faithfulness.

Roger did his best to address each grievance and promised to present Canonicus's case to the English Governors. For Roger's sake, and through the wisdom and sincerity of his pleas, the aged Chieftain declared himself satisfied. He broke off the Pequot negotiations and agreed instead to an alliance with the Bay!

When war between the Pequots and the English broke out

CANONICUS PICKED UP A STICK AND BROKE IT.

later that year, Miantonomy and the Narragansett braves fought on the side of the Bay. The Pequots were defeated and were never again a threat to any man.

God had used Roger to bring about a victory that enabled the whole land, English and natives, to sleep in peace securely. And though the Bay blessed God for Roger's unselfish courage and service to them in the conflict, his unrepentant Separatism would forever keep them apart. The banishment was not lifted.

THE PEQUOTS WERE DEFEATED.

NEW TOWNS SPRUNG UP.

11
A.D. 1637-1650
A Brief Minute

The years following the Pequot War saw Providence beginning to swell with an influx of new settlers: Seekers, Separatists, Baptists, Dissidents, and the Discontent. Roger purchased more land from Canonicus, including the Islands of Rhode and Aquidneck in the Narragansett Bay, and he tried to divvy it up equally to all who came.

But Winthrop's prediction of trouble rang all too true. Many who came to Roger's spiritual haven were far more concerned for themselves than for any great godly principles. They were more interested in license than in liberty. They were more intent on building their personal kingdoms than in seeking the Kingdom of God.

There were constant squabbles over the land. New towns (Newport, Pawtuxet and Portsmouth) sprung up, with their own governments, simply because folks couldn't get along. Roger was continually busy being "Moses" to a band of grumbling "Israelites."

He wrote often to Winthrop, who was Governor once

again, sharing his concerns and asking for advice. Winthrop did all that he could to help Roger "build his house on rock," but he was sincerely troubled by the growing community of spiritual oddballs and doctrinal outlaws.

Meanwhile, Massachussets, Plymouth, and Connecticut all began to look longingly southward toward the fertile, unchartered lands upon which Roger had settled. Within Roger's own borders, a man named William Arnold carved a large piece of Roger's pie for himself, and then gave it to Massachusetts!

If the new settlements south of the Seekonk were to survive as an independent colony alongside the older English plantations, they must have something more than land deeds from the Indians (which the English did not recognize as legal). They must have a Royal Charter. The Assembly at Newport voted to look into the possibility of an English patent for Rhode Island and the lands adjacent. Their choice of an agent to be sent to England on their behalf was, of course, Roger Williams.

❖

Roger bid farewell to his family and friends and set sail for England in March of 1643. During his voyage he wrote a

THE OTHER ENGLISH COLONIES WANTED ROGER'S LAND.

small book about the Narragansett Indians and their language and customs. He named it *A Key into the Language of America*. He compiled it as a help to his own memory and to many who had asked him for assistance in their temporal and spiritual dealings with the Natives. It was published in London upon his arrival in September, and became an instant hit, making Roger famous overnight.

Parliament had been reinstated by King Charles, and then dissolved by him a second time. Parliament then reconvened itself on behalf of the people of England and proceeded to declare war against their King. The civil war had begun only a year earlier in 1642, making it very difficult for Roger to find a listening ear for his problems across the seas. So he bided his time by entering the religious and political fray. He wrote many pamphlets in support of freedom of religion and against persecution for one's faith. He argued for an English government that encouraged differences in matters of faith, but that kept its hands out of Church matters. He argued for a Church that was pure and holy, and that kept itself free from the influence of the world. And he argued for a truce between the two that would allow all Englishmen to worship as their consciences dictated.

BACK IN ENGLAND, ROGER ENTERED
THE RELIGIOUS AND POLITICAL FRAY.

ROGER WILLIAMS

He wrote: "In many ways (not spiritual), the Church or gathering of worshipers, whether it is a True Church or not, is like a Physician's Society, a Merchant's Company, an East-Indies Tea Corporation, or any other society or company in London. Each of these societies holds its own meetings, keeps its own records, and goes about the concerns of its business. Its members may disagree, divide, form separate companies, sue each other at law, even break up and dissolve into nothing, and still the peace of the City is not in the least disturbed."

Surely a church can be allowed to operate in the same way, said Roger. Let each church, whether a true church or not, declare its own purposes and judge its own affairs. As to the Truth itself, it does not need the protection of the sword, nor can it be furthered by the sword. God's Spirit alone can reveal it, and God's power alone will preserve it! For God is Truth."

Most people thought this reasoning very strange, but Roger's words challenged them to reexamine their understanding of both Church and State. Roger was primarily arguing for the purity of the Church of Jesus Christ, and he had no way of knowing that he was also helping to lay the

ROGER'S WORDS MADE PEOPLE THINK!

foundation for a freer, more democratic society that would one day come forth in England and (much sooner) in America.

Finally, in March of 1644, Parliament granted Roger an official charter to Providence Plantations.

❖

In September of 1644, Roger was jubilantly welcomed home to Providence. The general outpouring of affection and appreciation warmed his heart, but it was tempered by the tragic news that his friend Miantonomy had been murdered by the Mohicans shortly after Roger had left for England.

"A giant has fallen," Roger murmured as he heard the grisly tale, and his mind wandered back to a day in his childhood, the day Bartholemew Legate was burned. As he had wondered then whether the heretic Legate had gone to Heaven or to Hell, so now he was burdened with fear for the eternal destiny of Miantonomy's soul. How he hated the barbaric spirit and fierce pride that held so many of the Natives in chains of darkness! He could almost hear his father's words: "Though I hate his heresy for the heresy it is. . ." Heresy or heathenism, what is the difference? Both lead to weeping and wailing and gnashing of teeth in the world beyond this one. ". . .he has been a *friend!*" A friend. A true friend.

"A GIANT HAS FALLEN."

Had Roger's friend Miantonomy ever truly trusted in Christ? Would he ever see his friend again?

The whole town assembled to hear the reading of the charter. After much public and private discussion, Providence accepted it as written, and Roger was immediately elected as Chief Officer of the new colony. The other three towns were much slower in agreeing to a unified government: it took them three years! But in May of 1647, all four towns finally organized themselves into one united body. Roger, feeling his part in the political salvation of the colony had been fully played, breathed a thankful sigh of relief, turned in his resignation, and headed for the woods. He was forty-four years old.

❖

Canonicus was fading fast. The brave old Prince had seen his last sunrise, and had sent a messenger running to Roger early in the day.

"I have asked my white son to close my eyes in death," Canonicus said feebly to the men and women who stood by his bed. "But I had hoped to see him once again before that hour."

Turning to the Sachem who would rule after him,

CANONICUS WAS FADING FAST.

Canonicus gave this charge, "Live with Roger Williams in love and in peace all your days. If war should ever come with the English, see that no Narragansett ever harm a hair of Roger's head."

When Roger arrived in the early evening, the women and the girls were wailing, their faces and clothes blackened with soot. The men lay weeping on thick piles of darkened ashes. The mournful cries of "Kitonckquêi! (He is dead!)" and "Nipwì mâw! (He is gone!)" could be heard throughout the city.

Roger walked solemnly into the death chamber of Canonicus. With unrestrained tears streaming down his cheeks, he looked one last time into the dark, vacant eyes of the great Chieftain. As an assembly of mourners gathered around, Roger gently placed his fingers on the eyelids of the dead Sachem. With one motion, he closed those eyes that had been open for so long and had seen so much. They had seen the birth and death of many sons and daughters. They had seen the rise and fall of many Indian nations. They had seen the coming of the White Man's ships. They had seen, and understood, the beginning of the end of the Narragansetts themselves.

ROGER CLOSED THOSE EYES
THAT HAD BEEN OPEN FOR SO LONG.

Roger rose, and the mourners fell weeping upon the mats within the wigwam.

"How dreadful is the death of the unbelieving," muttered Roger as he wandered back into the forest toward his home. "And yet, when the hearts of my countrymen and friends failed me, God's infinite wisdom and merits stirred up the barbarous heart of Canonicus to love me as his son to his last gasp."

❖

In a small, sunlit clearing about six miles from Providence, Roger built his trading house. Within sight of the sturdy log house was a quiet cove where a small pinnace was anchored. Pulled up on the shore were several smaller boats and canoes.

Many trails lead inland to the neighboring Indian villages (with twenty villages to a mile in some cases), and Roger's little house was constantly humming with the healthy activity of frontier trade.

For the Indians, Roger kept a full stock of everything they needed: pans, kettles, knives, cooking utensils of all sorts, spades, hoes, and other gardening equipment, cloth, pins, needles, thread, beads, trinkets, and toys. But the items in largest demand were tobacco and pipes to smoke it in.

ROGER'S TRADING HOUSE

Nobody then knew, as we now do, that tobacco was dangerous, and so Roger had a ready supply at all times. The one thing he would not carry, that the Natives craved even over tobacco, was whiskey. Though he could have made a fortune (as other less scrupulous traders did) in the sale of alcohol, he loved the Indians too much to sell them something that could destroy them.

Though these were busy days for Roger, it was a quiet sort of busyness. And though his trading post and his farm in Providence provided well for his household, the trading post also provided something far nearer his heart: a pulpit from which to preach. "Preaching is the best of all callings," Roger said, "but a poor trade." So he did both. His Indian customers were his parish, and he preached to them often. And not just on Sundays.

Sometimes Roger's wife Mary would come from their home in Providence to be with him and help him in his work. Sometimes his two oldest daughters, Mary and Freeborn, would be with him (there were now six Williams children growing up in the Providence home). Sometimes he labored alone. During this time he wrote a little spiritual devotional for his wife, entitled *Experiments of Spiritual Life and Health*.

TRADING WAS A QUIET SORT OF BUSYNESS FOR ROGER.

Unlike most of his other writings, it was not at all controversial and was full of practical encouragement for living the Christian life.

❖

In the year 1649, two great men died.

One died an old man, peacefully in his bed in the New World, leaving behind him a legacy of godliness, temperance, and a spiritual, moral, and governmental foundation upon which a unique and mighty nation would be built.

The other died in the prime of his life, violently on a scaffold in the Old World, leaving behind him a record of royal fortitude, personal courage, and a doomed struggle to revive an ancient, outmoded philosophy of English life.

The man in his bed was John Winthrop, and all of New England mourned his passing.

The man on the scaffold was King Charles the First, and though many rejoiced at his fall, much of England groaned. More was severed than the King's neck with the swift blow of the executioner's axe. Broken forever in that instant was England's unthinking submission to the Crown. What England's new leader, Oliver Cromwell, called "cruel necessity" was the dim beginning of a society governed by the

IN THE YEAR 1649, TWO GREAT MEN DIED.

people and for the people. But it was a harsh genesis. And it was a long crawl toward true freedom. England's Puritans now had the chance to rule in Old England. It wouldn't be easy.

In Providence, Roger wept for the passing of the man in Boston. Though Winthrop had been among those who had banished him, the two had been through much together. Roger would miss him dearly, though they would meet again in a longer, brighter day. He wept also for the death of the man in London, for he knew the man's deeds had been wicked.

Both men would stand before God to give an account for their lives.

"This life is but a brief minute" said Roger quietly. "Eternity follows."

"LIFE IS BUT A BRIEF MINUTE. ETERNITY FOLLOWS."

IT WAS A BLACK PAGE IN NEW ENGLAND HISTORY.

12
A.D. 1675
King Philip's War

It was a black page in New England history. A war of shame for both red man and white. Fear and distrust, self-righteousness and revenge, ruled in men's hearts. Prudence and promises were trampled underfoot as drums beat and and arrows flew and muskets bellowed.

Much blood was shed, and much of it innocent blood—blood of Indian and Englishman alike. But all of it red as it soaked the common soil.

English settlers were killed in their sleep, whole families massacred. Homes were burned. Towns were burned. Cattle was destroyed. Crops were ravaged.

Indian warriors and helpless old men and women were slaughtered in a tragic winter battle that needn't have been fought. The Narragansett tribe was reduced to near extinction.

In Rhode Island (as Providence Plantation was now called), Roger desperately tried to convince the pacifist Quaker government of Providence to fortify the town. But they would not. The town of Warwick was burned on March 17, and on March 26, the marauding Wampanoag Indians arrived at

Providence.

As the Native force approached the town, they were met by a white-haired seventy-three year old man who was leaning on a staff. He called out to them, saying that he would parley with them. They spoke with him for an hour, but he was unable to dissuade them from their dreadful purpose. Roger Williams's influence meant nothing on that fatal day. Most of Providence, including Roger's home and all his worldly goods, was burned to the ground. Only twenty-three houses out of a hundred and three remained. But no one touched as much of a hair on Roger's head.

Four months later, King Philip (Metacomet, son of Massasoit), the bitter Sachem who had incited and led the massive Indian uprising, was slain in a swamp by a former member of his tribe. Sixteen days later the war ended at Annawan Rock on the eastern side of the Seekonk River.

New England would rise again from the ashes, stronger and more determined than ever to follow its destiny to the ends of an empire. Not so the tribes that had filled its tall forests; they would diminish as the years went by, like trees growing backwards from maturity to saplings, and then to mere seeds lost amidst the rocks and ferns.

ROGER'S INFLUENCE MEANT NOTHING THAT FATAL DAY.

"ROGER WILLIAMS IS DEAD," THEY SAID.

13
A.D. 1683
Eternity Pays All

"Mary," said Roger weakly.

"Yes, dearest,"whispered his tender wife and faithful companion.

"Have you anything you wish me to say to Winthrop when I see him?" asked Roger.

"To Winthrop?" said Mary hesitantly. Then she laughed gently, for surely Roger was dreaming. Old John Winthrop had been dead for over thirty years. But then her face grew solemn, and she stood up from her chair and walked over to the bed where Roger lay.

"Roger," she said sadly and softly. "Tell him he was wrong."

❖

"Kitonckquêi," they said, in the depleted villages of the Narragansetts. And those who had known him smeared themselves with soot.

"He is dead," they said, in the towns and on the trails of

New England. And those who had known him bowed their heads in prayer.

"Oh, how terrible is the look, the speedy and serious thought of death to all the sons of men!" he himself once wrote. "Thrice happy are those who are dead and risen with the Son of God, for they are passed from death to life, and shall never see death again!"

❖

The town of Providence turned out in unison in a vast parade that followed Roger's body to its burial. A final loud salute was raised as guns were fired over the grave. Red and white, Christian and Jew, heretic and and heathen: all stood together on the hallowed ground. Some wept. Some wondered. Their united peaceful presence there was all the honor Roger would have wished for.

GLOSSARY

Anglican: English.

Anglican Church: the name of the official church of England, first formed when King Henry VIII separated from the Roman Catholic Church in the 16th century.

commoner *or* **common man**: the classes of English citizens who were not of noble or royal rank or birth. The commoners had fewer rights and privileges than the nobles.

doctrine: the truths of the Bible, or the beliefs of a particular church.

heretic: a person who rejects or denies the revealed truths of the Bible; especially, a person who teaches false ideas about the Bible.

hove: when a ship or boat has been moved in a certain direction.

martyr: a person who voluntarily suffers death rather than renounce his religious beliefs.

merchant taylor: a buyer and seller of imported cloth (not one who manufactures or repairs clothing).

Merchant Taylors' Company: the London trade association of merchant taylors.

parley: to discuss terms of war or peace with an enemy.

Parliament: a formal assembly for the discussion of public affairs and for the recommendation and passing of laws.

Puritan: any English Protestant who opposed unbiblical and ceremonial practices and teachings within the Anglican Church.

persecution: harassing, hurting, or imposing hardship and suffering on someone because of their religious beliefs.

Sachem: chief of an Indian village, tribe, or nation.

Separatist: any English Protestant who believed that it was best to totally separate from the Anglican Church rather than stay in it and reform it.

In all books, there are bound to be unfamiliar words. It's a good idea to keep a dictionary nearby whenever you read a new book. If you come to a word that you don't understand, grab your dictionary and look it up!

HARRAP'S
MINI POCKET
DICTIONARY

HARRAP'S
MINI POCKET
DICTIONARY

French-English/English-French

ABRIDGED BY

PATRICIA FORBES, B.A. (Oxon)

AND

MARGARET LEDÉSERT, M.A.

FROM
*Harrap's New Shorter French
and English Dictionary*

HARRAP LONDON

First published as
Harrap's New Pocket French and English Dictionary
in 1969

First published in this edition
in Great Britain 1977
by HARRAP LIMITED
19–23 Ludgate Hill London EC4M 7PD

Reprinted 1977; 1978; 1979; 1980; 1981; 1982;
1983; 1984

ISBN 0 245-53135-1 (*Great Britain*)
ISBN 2-04-010130-6 (*France*)
ISBN 0 8442 1871 5 (*United States*)

Printed in Great Britain by
Richard Clay (The Chaucer Press) Ltd,
Bungay, Suffolk

PREFACE

THIS work is a completely new version of HARRAP'S POCKET FRENCH AND ENGLISH DICTIONARY, originally compiled by the late R. P. Jago, and aims at offering the user a useful modern vocabulary of French and English words, including French-Canadianisms, Americanisms and Australianisms. The main body of the work does not include place names or proper names, which are listed in separate appendices.

As far as the English language is concerned, the standard spellings current in England have been used throughout. Common alternative spellings are given in the English-French part, though it should be noted that for words with the alternate suffixes -ise or -ize and -isation or -ization, -ize and -ization have been adopted throughout. The attention of the North-American user is directed towards a few salient differences in spelling:

(a) the English use of -our in words which in American usage are spelt with -or (*e.g. Eng:* colour, *U.S:* color).

(b) the use of the final -re in words where American usage favours -er (*e.g. Eng:* theatre, *U.S:* theater).

(c) the doubling of the l before an ending beginning with a vowel, irrespective of accentuation (*e.g. Eng:* woollen, *U.S:* woolen; *Eng:* travelling, *U.S:* traveling).

(d) the single l before a final syllable beginning with a consonant, where the American usage is ll (*e.g. Eng:* skilful, *U.S:* skillful; *Eng:* enrolment, *U.S:* enrollment).

(e) the use of a c in certain words where American usage favours an s (*e.g. Eng:* defence, *U.S:* defense).

The phonetics of both French and English words are given according to the symbols of the International Phonetic Association

An outstanding feature of the dictionary is the number of examples given to show the various uses of the more important words. In order to do this and to keep the length to reasonable dimensions a number of space-saving devices have been adopted:

1. When in an example a headword is repeated in exactly the same form it is represented by the initial letter, though plural nouns or

Preface

verb conjugations in which the form differs from the infinitive are given in full.

e.g. **pave**, *v.tr.* paver (une rue) . . . **to p. the way**, préparer le terrain.

2. In the French-English part a certain number of adverbs and simple derivatives follow the headword; the form of these is indicated simply by the ending and no translation is given if no difficulty in meaning is involved. *e.g.* **prison**, *s.f.* prison. *s.* -nier, -nière, prisoner; **observ/er**, *v.tr.* to observe . . . . *s.f.* -ation.

3. In the English-French part nouns, verbs, adjectives or adverbs which have the same form are shown together under one headword, with the distinguishing divisions **I, II, III**, etc. Derivatives, whether hyphenated or not, are listed under the main headword, but the words appear in full in order that the stressed syllable may be shown.

e.g. **peel**, I. *s.* pelure *f* . . . **II.** *v.* **1.** *v.tr.* peler (un fruit) . . . ′**peeler**, *s.* éplucheur *m* . . . ′**peelings**, *s.pl.* épluchures *f*.

Derivatives appear in alphabetical order with the exception of adverbs, which are usually designated as -ly, -ily, etc., and which come immediately after the adjective.

The following conventions have also been observed:

(*a*) Nouns have been described as 'substantives', being listed as *s.m.* or *s.f.* in the French-English part. In the English-French part the gender is given after the French word. Nouns which have irregular plurals, or French adjectives with irregular plurals or feminine forms are marked †; for these words the user should refer to the grammar notes at the beginning of each part. An exception to this rule is made for French hyphenated nouns; as the rules governing the plurals are complicated the plural is given under the headword. The user is therefore advised to consult the French headword for the plural of a compound noun occurring in the translation in the English/French part.

(*b*) Irregular verbs are marked ‡, and for these also the user should refer to the grammar notes.

(*c*) Owing to the different systems of administration, etc., in the different countries it is not always possible to give true translations for different functions or offices. In such cases the sign = has been used to indicate the nearest equivalent.

We should like to thank all who have helped us in our revision work and in the reading of the proofs, notably Mr R. P. L. Ledésert, *Licencié en Droit, Licencié ès Lettres*, Miss M. Holland Smith, Mr F. G. S. Parker, M.A., Mrs F. Collin, M.A. (Montréal), Mr P. H. Collin, M.A., Mrs E. A. H. Strick, M.A., and Mr R. Usher, M.B.E., M.A.

Patricia Forbes
Margaret Ledésert

PRÉFACE

CET ouvrage est une version entièrement nouvelle du HARRAP'S POCKET FRENCH AND ENGLISH DICTIONARY, par R. P. Jago, dont le but est d'offrir à l'usager un vocabulaire utile et moderne du français et de l'anglais, y compris de nombreux canadianismes français, des américanismes et des mots utilisés en Australie. Nous n'avons donné ni noms géographiques ni noms propres dans l'ouvrage même mais ceux-ci figurent dans des appendices.

L'orthographe des mots anglais respecte l'usage britannique. Les variantes usuelles figurent dans la partie anglais-français; il faut cependant signaler que pour la double forme des suffixes -ise ou -ize, et -isation ou -ization l'orthographe -ize et -ization a été adoptée dans les deux parties du dictionnaire.

Nous attirons l'attention du lecteur habitué à l'usage américain sur quelques différences particulièrement frappantes:

(a) l'emploi anglais de -our dans des mots pour lesquels l'américain emploierait l'orthographe -or (ex. angl: colour, U.S: color).

(b) l'emploi de la finale -re dans des mots pour lesquels l'usage américain donne la préférence à la forme -er (ex. angl: theatre, U.S: theater).

(c) le redoublement de la lettre l devant une voyelle (ex. angl: woollen, U.S: woolen; angl: travelling, U.S: traveling).

(d) l'emploi de l'l simple devant une syllabe finale commençant par une consonne, alors que l'usage américain est ll (ex. angl: skilful, U.S: skillful; angl: enrolment, U.S: enrollment).

(e) l'emploi d'un c dans certains mots pour lesquels l'américain donne la préférence à l's (ex. angl: defence, U.S: defense).

Pour la transcription phonétique des mots français et anglais, nous employons les signes de l'Association phonétique internationale.

Les nombreux exemples donnés pour illustrer l'usage des mots les plus importants est l'une des caractéristiques essentielles de ce dictionnaire. Cependant, afin d'éviter d'accroître démesurément le volume de l'ouvrage un certain nombre de règles typographiques ont été adoptées pour gagner de la place.

Préface

1. Quand, dans un exemple, un mot principal est répété sans changement, il est représenté par la lettre initiale, alors que les noms au pluriel ou les formes des verbes pour lesquels l'orthographe change (ce qui n'est pas toujours le cas en anglais), sont écrites en toutes lettres. *ex.* pave, *v.tr.* paver (une rue) . . . to p. the way, préparer le terrain.

2. Dans la partie français-anglais un certain nombre d'adverbes et de dérivés simples sont insérés à la suite du mot principal, avec ou sans traduction suivant la difficulté de la traduction. *ex.* prison, *s.f.* prison. *s.* -nier, -nière, prisoner; observ/er, *v.tr.* to observe . . . *s.f.* -ation.

3. Dans la partie anglais-français les noms, verbes, adjectifs ou adverbes ayant la même forme sont groupés sous le même mot principal, et séparés par les sous-titres I, II, III, etc. Les dérivés, écrits avec ou sans trait d'union, suivent le mot principal; ils sont écrits en toutes lettres afin de pouvoir indiquer la syllabe accentuée. *ex.* peel. I. *s.* pelure *f* . . . II. *v.* 1. *v.tr.* peler (un fruit) . . . 'peeler, *s.* éplucheur *m* . . . 'peelings, *s.pl.* épluchures *f.*

Les dérivés sont placés par ordre alphabétique, à l'exception des adverbes en -ly, qui suivent directement les adjectifs.

En outre, les conventions suivantes one été respectées:

(*a*) Les noms ont été classés comme substantifs et leur genre défini *s.m.* ou *s.f.* dans la partie français-anglais. Dans la partie anglais-français le genre est indiqué après le mot français. Les noms dont le pluriel est irrégulier et les adjectifs français, dont le féminin ou le pluriel ne se forme pas par la simple addition d'un -e ou d'un -s sont accompagnés du signe † qui renvoie le lecteur aux notes grammaticales placées au début de chaque partie, français-anglais et anglais-français. Une exception à cette règle générale est faite pour les noms composés français, dont le pluriel suit le mot principal en raison des règles compliquées qui régissent le pluriel de ces noms.

(*b*) Les verbes irréguliers sont indiqués par le signe ‡ qui renvoie le lecteur aux notes grammaticales.

(*c*) Etant donné les différences dans les structures administratives et autres des deux pays, il n'est pas toujours possible de traduire exactement les diverses charges, fonctions, etc. Dans de tels cas, le signe = a été utilisé pour indiquer l'équivalent le plus proche.

Nous tenons à remercier tous ceux qui nous ont aidées au travail de révision et à la lecture des épreuves: Mr R. P. L. Ledésert, *Licencié en Droit, Licencié-ès-Lettres*, Miss M. Holland Smith, Mr F. G. S. Parker, M.A., Mrs F. Collin, M.A. (Montréal), Mr P. H. Collin, M.A., Mrs E. A. H. Strick, M.A., et Mr R. Usher, M.B.E., M.A.

Patricia Forbes
Margaret Ledésert

8

ABBREVIATIONS
USED IN THE DICTIONARY

a.	adjective	adjectif
A. & A:	art and architecture	beaux arts et architecture
abs.	absolute use of verb	emploi absolu du verbe
Adm:	administration	administration
adv.	adverb	adverbe
Agr:	agriculture	agriculture
Anat:	anatomy	anatomie
approx.	approximately	sens approché
art.	article	article
Atom Ph:	atomic physics	sciences atomiques
Austr:	Australia; Australian	Australie; australien
Aut:	cars, motoring	automobilisme, voitures
aux.	auxiliary	auxiliaire
Av:	aviation, aircraft, aeronautics	aviation, avions, aéronautique
Bot:	botany	botanique
Can:	Canada; Canadian	Canada; canadien
Ch:	chemistry	chimie
Cin:	cinema	cinéma
Civ.E:	civil engineering	génie civil
Cl:	clothing	vêtements
coll.	collective	collectif
Com:	commerce	commerce
comp.	comparative	comparatif
conj.	conjunction	conjonction
Cu:	cooking, food	cuisine, comestibles
def.	definite	défini
dem.	demonstrative	démonstratif
E:	engineering, mechanics	mécanique, industries mécaniques
Ecc:	ecclesiastical	église et clergé
El:	electricity	électricité
Eng:	English; England	Angleterre; anglais
esp.	especially	surtout
etc:	et cetera	et cætera
excl.	exclamation, exclamatory	exclamation, exclamatif
f.	feminine	féminin
F:	colloquial	familier
Fb:	football and rugby	football et rugby
Fin:	finance	finances
Fish:	fish; fishing	poissons; pêche
Fr:	French; France	français; France
Fr. C:	French Canadian	canadien français
fu.	future	futur
Geog:	geography	géographie
Gram:	grammar	grammaire
H:	household	économie domestique
Her:	heraldry	blason
Hist:	history	histoire
imp.	imperative	impératif
imperf.	imperfect	imparfait
impers.	impersonal	impersonnel
Ind:	industry, industrial	industrie, industriel
indef.	indefinite	indéfini
interrog.	interrogative	interrogatif
inv.	invariable	invariable
Jur:	law	droit, terme du palais
Ling:	linguistics	linguistique
Lit:	literary use; literature	forme littéraire, littérature
m.	masculine	masculin
Med:	medicine	médecine
Meteo:	meteorology	météorologie
Mil:	military	militaire

Abbreviations

Min:	minerals; mining	minéraux; minerais; exploitation des mines
Mth:	mathematics	mathématiques
Mus:	music	musique
Nau:	nautical; navy	terme nautique; marine
neg.	negative	négatif
occ.	occasionally	parfois
p.	(*i*) participle, (*ii*) past	(*i*) participe, (*ii*) passé
P:	uneducated expression, slang	populaire, argot
Pej:	pejorative	péjoratif
pers.	person; personal	personne; personnel
Ph:	physics	physique
Phot:	photography	photographie
pl.	plural	pluriel
P.N:	public notice	avis au public
Pol:	politics	politique
poss.	possessive	possessif
p.p.	past participle	participe passé
pred.	predicative	attributif
prep.	preposition	préposition
Pr. n.	proper name	nom propre
pron.	pronoun	pronom
pr. p.	present participle	participe présent
P.T.T:	post, telegraph, telephone	postes et télécommunications
Psy:	psychology	psychologie
qch.	(something)	quelque chose
qn	(someone)	quelqu'un
Rad:	radio	radio
Rail:	railways	chemins de fer
Rec:	gramophones, tape-recording	phonographes, magnétophones
rel.	relative	relatif
R.t.m.	registered trade mark	marque déposée
s.	noun	substantif
Sc:	science	sujets scientifiques
Sch:	scholastic	scolaire
Scot:	Scotland; Scottish	Écosse; écossais
sg.	singular	singulier
s.o.	someone	(quelqu'un)
Sp:	sport, games	sport, jeux
sth.	something	(quelque chose)
sub.	subjunctive	subjonctif
Techn:	technical terms	terme(s) technique(s), de métier
Th:	theatre	théâtre
T.V:	television	télévision
U.S:	United States; American	États-Unis; américain
usu.	usually	d'ordinaire
v.	verb	verbe
v.i.	intransitive verb	verbe intransitif
v. ind. tr.	verb indirectly transitive	verb transitif indirect
v. pr.	pronominal (reflexive) verb	verbe pronominal
v. tr.	transitive verb	verbe transitif
Z:	zoology	zoologie

PART I
FRENCH-ENGLISH: FRANÇAIS-ANGLAIS

GRAMMAR NOTES

I. FEMININE AND PLURAL FORMS

1. General rules: To form the feminine of an adjective, add -e; if the masculine form ends in -e, the feminine form is the same as the masculine. *N.B.* If the adjective ends in -é, -e is added to form the feminine, *e.g.* carré, carrée. To form the plural of a noun or adjective, add -s to the singular form; if the noun or adjective ends in -s, -x, or -z, the plural form is the same as the singular. Adjectives and nouns which do not follow these general rules are marked †, and the summaries below give the principal rules governing these.

2. Irregular feminines of adjectives

(*a*) masculine ending -if, feminine -ive. *e.g.* actif, active; vif, vive.

(*b*) masculine ending -eux, feminine -euse. *e.g.* heureux, heureuse. *Exception:* vieux, *f.* vieille, *m.* form before vowel sound vieil.

(*c*) masculine ending -eau or -ou, feminine -elle, -olle; *m.* ending before vowel sound -el, -ol. *e.g.* beau, bel, belle; nouveau, nouvel, nouvelle; fou, fol, folle. *N.B.* No alternative *m* form for jumeau, as this adjective always comes after the noun it qualifies.

(*d*) masculine ending -er, feminine -ère; some adjectives ending in -et also add the grave accent. *e.g.* léger, légère; premier, première; complet, complète; discret, discrète; incomplet, incomplète; inquiet, inquiète; secret, secrète.

(*e*) for most adjectives ending in -l, -n, -s, and -t, double the consonant and add -e to form the feminine. *e.g.* cruel, cruelle; gentil, gentille; nul, nulle; gras, grasse; gros, grosse; las, lasse; muet, muette; net, nette; sot, sotte; bon, bonne. *Note also:* faux, fausse; roux, rousse.

(*f*) masculine ending -u, feminine -uë. *e.g.* aigu, aiguë; ambigu, ambiguë.

(*g*) for irregular adjectives which are also nouns, the feminine form is given under the headword, *e.g.* pécheur, consolateur.

(*h*) irregular forms not in the above categories: bénin, bénigne; blanc, blanche; favori, favorite; franc, franche; grec, grecque; long, longue; malin, maligne; public, publique; sec, sèche; turc, turque.

3. Plurals of nouns and adjectives

(*a*) for most nouns or adjectives ending in -au or -eu, add -x, to form the plural. *e.g.* manteau, manteaux; jumeau, jumeaux; eau, eaux;

13

Grammar notes

cheveu, cheveux. *Exceptions:* bleu, bleus; pneu, pneus; landau, landaus.

(*b*) singular -al, plural -aux. *e.g.* cheval, chevaux; journal, journaux; loyal, loyaux; mal, maux. *Exceptions:* bal, bals; banal, banals; carnaval, carnavals; chacal, chacals; naval, navals; fatal, fatals; glacial, glacials; régal, régals; the plural of idéal is usually idéaux, but sometimes idéals.

(*c*) most nouns ending in -ou, plural -ous: *e.g.* trou, trous. *Exceptions:* bijou, bijoux; caillou, cailloux; chou, choux; genou, genoux; hibou, hiboux; pou, poux.

(*d*) for a few nouns ending in -ail, plural form -aux: bail, baux; corail, coraux; émail, émaux; soupirail, soupiraux; travail, travaux; vitrail, vitraux; the plural of ail is aulx or ails.

(*e*) nouns with highly irregular or double plurals: (*i*) aïeul, aïeuls (= *great-grandparents*), aïeux (= *ancestors*); (*ii*) ciel, cieux, but ciels in meaning of skies in a painting; (*iii*) œil, yeux.

(*f*) as the rules are complicated, the plurals of hyphenated nouns are given under the headwords.

(*g*) Note the following plurals (originally written as two words): madame, mesdames; mademoiselle, mesdemoiselles; monsieur, messieurs; monseigneur, messeigneurs.

(*h*) qualified colour adjectives are invariable: *e.g.* une robe gris clair; des yeux blue foncé.

II. VERB CONJUGATION

1. Regular verbs

Infinitive	-ER Verbs donn/er	-IR Verbs fin/ir	-RE Verbs vend/re
1. Present	je donne	je finis	je vends
	tu donnes	tu finis	tu vends
	il donne	il finit	il vend
	nous donnons	nous finissons	nous vendons
	vous donnez	vous finissez	vous vendez
	ils donnent	ils finissent	ils vendent
2. Imperfect	je donnais	je finissais	je vendais
	tu donnais	tu finissais	tu vendais
	il donnait	il finissait	il vendait
	nous donnions	nous finissions	nous vendions
	vous donniez	vous finissiez	vous vendiez
	ils donnaient	ils finissaient	ils vendaient
3. Past Historic	je donnai	je finis	je vendis
	tu donnas	tu finis	tu vendis
	il donna	il finit	il vendit
	nous donnâmes	nous finîmes	nous vendîmes
	vous donnâtes	vous finîtes	vous vendîtes
	ils donnèrent	ils finirent	ils vendirent
4. Future	je donnerai	je finirai	je vendrai
	tu donneras	tu finiras	tu vendras
	il donnera	il finira	il vendra
	nous donnerons	nous finirons	nous vendrons
	vous donnerez	vous finirez	vous vendrez
	ils donneront	ils finiront	ils vendront

14

Grammar notes

5. Present Subjunctive	je donne	je finisse	je vende
	tu donnes	tu finisses	tu vendes
	il donne	il finisse	il vende
	nous donnions	nous finissions	nous vendions
	vous donniez	vous finissiez	vous vendiez
	ils donnent	ils finissent	ils vendent
6. Imperative	donne	finis	vends
	donnons	finissons	vendons
	donnez	finissez	vendez
7. Present Participle	donnant	finissant	vendant
8. Past Participle	donné	fini	vendu

The table above shows the conjugation of the principal tenses of the three main groups of verbs. Among the -er verbs there are some slight modifications which do not qualify the verbs in question to be classified as irregular, and which are listed below.

(a) verbs in -ger (e.g. **manger**) *All* these verbs take an extra e before endings beginning with o or a.

Present: je mange, nous mangeons; *Imperfect:* je mangeais, nous mangions; *Past Historic:* je mangeai, etc.; *Present participle:* mangeant.

(b) verbs in -cer (e.g. **commencer**) *All* these verbs change c to ç before endings beginning with o or a. *Present:* je commence, nous commençons; *Imperfect:* je commençais, nous commencions; *Past Historic:* je commençai, etc.; *Present Participle:* commençant.

(c) When the infinitive ends in e + **single consonant** + er (e.g. **appeler, acheter**) the verbs fall into two groups:

(i) some (e.g. **appeler**) double the consonant before the unpronounced endings of the present tense, and in the future: *Present:* j'appelle, nous appelons, ils appellent; *Future:* j'appellerai. Like **appeler**: atteler; épeler; épousseter; renouveler.

(ii) Others (e.g. **acheter**) add a grave accent. *Present:* J'achète, nous achetons, ils achètent. *Future:* j'achèterai. Like **acheter**: congeler; dégeler; geler; mener; modeler; peler; peser.

(d) When the infinitive ends in é + **single consonant** + er (e.g. **espérer**) the acute accent changes to grave in the present tense, but the acute accent is maintained in the future.

Present: j'espère, nous espérons, ils espèrent. *Future* j'espérerai.

(e) Verbs in -yer (e.g. **essuyer**) The y changes to i before the unpronounced endings of the present tense: j'essuie, nous essuyons; ils essuient: *Future:* j'essuierai.

2. Irregular verbs

Irregular verbs are listed alphabetically below. As verb endings in the imperfect, future and present subjunctive (with few exceptions) are

Grammar notes

invariable, and those of the past historic (with a few exceptions) fall into three groups, only the first person singular has been given for these tenses. For the present tense the first person singular and plural are generally adequate, though other persons are given for highly irregular verbs. The imperative is given only if it differs from the present tense. Only those tenses in which irregularities occur are listed; for other tenses see the type -ER, -IR, and -RE verbs.

1. = Present. 2. = Imperfect. 3. = Past historic. 4. = Future. 5. = Present subjunctive. 6. = Imperative. 7. = Present participle. 8. = Past participle. n. = nous. v. = vous. * verbs conjugated with être.

ABATTRE, *like* **battre.**   **ABSOUDRE.** 1. j'absous, n. absolvons; 2. j'absolvais; 3. *rarely used*; 5. j'absolve; 7. absolvant; 8. absous, absoute.   **ABSTRAIRE.** 1. j'abstrais, n. abstrayons; 2. j'abstrayais; 3. *none*; 5. j'abstraie; 7. abstrayant; 8. abstrait.   **ACQUÉRIR.** 1. j'acquiers, n. acquérons; 2. j'acquérais; 3. j'acquis; 4. j'acquer.ai; 5. j'acquière; 7. acquérant; 8. acquis.   **ACCUEILLIR,** *like* **cueillir.**   **ADJOINDRE,** *like* **atteindre.**   **ADMETTRE,** *like* **mettre.**   ***ALLER.** 1. je vais, tu vas, il va, n. allons, ils vont; 4. j'irai; 5. j'aille, nous allions, ils aillent; 6. va, allons, allez.   **APERCEVOIR,** *like* **recevoir.**   **APPARAÎTRE,** *like* **connaître.**   **APPARTENIR,** *like* **tenir.**   **APPRENDRE,** *like* **prendre.**   **ASSEOIR.** 1. j'assieds, n. asseyons, ils asseyent; 2. j'asseyais; 3. j'assis; 4. j'assiérai; 5. j'asseye; 7. asseyant; 8. assis. (*similarly * s'asseoir*).   **ASTREINDRE,** *like* **atteindre.**   **ATTEINDRE.** 1. j'atteins; n. atteignons, ils atteignent; 2. j'atteignais; 3. j'atteignis; 4. j'atteindrai; 5. j'atteigne; 7. atteignant; 8. atteint.   **AVOIR.** 1. j'ai, tu as, il a, n. avons, v. avez, ils ont; 2. j'avais; 3. j'eus; 4. j'aurai; 5. j'aie, il ait, n. ayons, ils aient; 6. aie, ayons, ayez; 7. ayant; 8. eu.   **BATTRE.** 1. je bats; n. battons; 5. je batte.   **BOIRE.** 1. je bois; n. buvons, ils boivent; 2. je buvais; 3. je bus; 5. je boive, n. buvions; 7. buvant; 8. bu.   **BOUILLIR.** 1. je bous, n. bouillons; 2. je bouillais; 3. *not used*; 5. je bouille; 7. bouillant.   **BRAIRE** (*defective*). 1. il brait, ils braient; 4. il braira, ils brairont.   **CIRCONCIRE.** 1. je circoncis; n. circoncisons; 3. je circoncis; 8. circoncis.   **CIRCONSCRIRE,** *like* **écrire.**   **CIRCONVENIR,** *like* **venir.**   **COMBATTRE,** *like* **battre.**   **COMMETTRE,** *like* **mettre.**   **COMPARAÎTRE,** *like* **connaître.**   **COMPRENDRE,** *like* **prendre.**   **COMPROMETTRE,** *like* **mettre.**   **CONCEVOIR,** *like* **recevoir.**   **CONCLURE.** 1. je conclue, n. concluons.   **CONCOURIR,** *like* **courir.**   **CONDUIRE.** 1. je conduis, n. conduisons; 3. je conduisis; 8. conduit.   **CONNAÎTRE.** 1. je connais, il connaît, n. connaissons; 3. je connus; 5. je connaisse; 7. connaissant; 8. connu.   **CONQUÉRIR,** *like* **acquérir.**   **CON-**

16